Diary of a Would-Be Princess

Diary of a Would-Be Princess

The Journal of Jillian James, 5B

Jessica Green

SCHOLASTIC

For Nicholas, Richard and Gillian.
JG

First published in Australia by Scholastic Australia Pty Ltd, 2005
This edition published in the UK by Scholastic Ltd, 2007
Scholastic Children's Books
An imprint of Scholastic Ltd
Euston House, 24 Eversholt Street
London, NW1 1DB, UK
Registered office: Westfield Road, Southam, Warwickshire, CV47 0RA
SCHOLASTIC and associated logos are trademarks and or registered
trademarks of Scholastic Inc.

Text copyright © Jessica Green, 2005
Cover illustration copyright © Jessie Eckel, 2007
The right of Jessica Green to be identified as the author of this work has
been asserted by her.

10 digit ISBN 0 439 95122 4
13 digit ISBN 978 0439 95122 7

British Library Cataloguing-in-Publication Data
A CIP catalogue record for this book is available from the British Library

Printed in the UK by CPI Bookmarque, Croydon, CR0 4TD
Papers used by Scholastic Children's Books are made from wood grown
in sustainable forests.

3 5 7 9 10 8 6 4

This is a work of fiction. Names, characters, places, incidents and
dialogues are products of the author's imagination or are used fictitiously.
Any resemblance to actual people, living or dead, events or locales is
entirely coincidental.

www.scholastic.co.uk/zone

Term One

Monday

My teacher says that to learn to dance, you dance and if you want to be a good singer, you sing. She's always telling us that. She has a poster on the wall that says:

TEN WAYS TO IMPROVE YOUR READING.
1. READ.
2. READ.
3. READ.
4. READ.
5. READ.
6. READ.
7. READ.
8. READ.
9. READ.
And 10. READ!

There are little pictures of koalas and kangaroos with their noses in books with titles like UNDERSTANDING HUMANS and EFFECTIVE TREE CLIMBING. The kids think it's funny. Mrs Bright loves it. She makes us read it out loud every day before we do Buddy Reading.

Now she's given us these exercise books. We have to make a title page with our name and JOURNAL written on it. We have to draw pictures of things we like, to show our interests and personalities. We have to do this in our free time. I have a problem with free time. I don't get any. I always have to do my maths again in free time.

Now I'm writing on the next page because Mrs Bright says we have to do Journal Writing EVERY day! Guess what she says?

If you want to be a good writer, you have to:

WRITE, WRITE, WRITE, WRITE, WRITE, WRITE, WRITE, WRITE, WRITE, WRITE!

The reason I'm writing now is so I can get out to recess. I can't wait to get out to the playground because we're going to swap friendship pins.

Tuesday

So much for friendship pins.

I spent hours and hours on Sunday while the football was on making mine. You have to get safety pins and beads. I found some pins in Paul's nappy and an old necklace in Mum's drawer. I didn't think she'd want it because she never wears it. The beads were black and white. I broke the string and made the pins. You have to pull the safety part off to thread the pins on and then put it back on. I made a really complicated pattern. Like this:

My brother Richard said it was an arithmetic pattern.

2-3-2-2-1-1-1-2-2-3-2.

I don't know what he means, but I'm hopeless at maths.

Yesterday we went to the Tree in the playground to give out our pins. I gave mine to Kirrily and Skye. Kirrily reckoned hers looked like a zebra. Skye wanted to know where I got the big pins. I told them and they screamed and dropped them. Then they tried to give their pins to Karlie and Sara. AND they told everyone about my pins and now they're all calling me Nappy Girl. AND Nigel picked up my pins and is wearing them and won't give them back.

I wish I was dead.

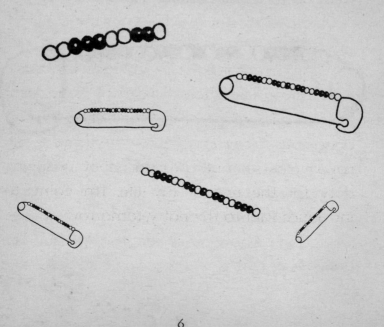

Wednesday

Yesterday was bad but today I REALLY wish I was dead. Yesterday afternoon Mum asked if anyone had seen her black and white fake pearl necklace because she wants to wear it on the weekend. Mum and Dad are going out for their anniversary.

Richard and I kept really quiet so Mum kept searching in all the drawers. Then she trod on a black bead I must have dropped. I said something about Paul liking necklaces so she went off to search his room. But just then the doorbell rang. Guess who was there? Nigel. Guess what he was wearing?

Now I'm grounded for two weeks. I have to re-thread every stupid pearl by Saturday. I have to apologize to Nigel for calling him an obnoxious creep and Mum says since I like nappy pins so much I'm on nappy changing duty for the rest of my life. I'm going to introduce Paul to the potty tomorrow.

Thursday

I thought yesterday was bad but today's worse. We're doing graphs in maths and now I can do line graphs. This is a graph of my life this week:

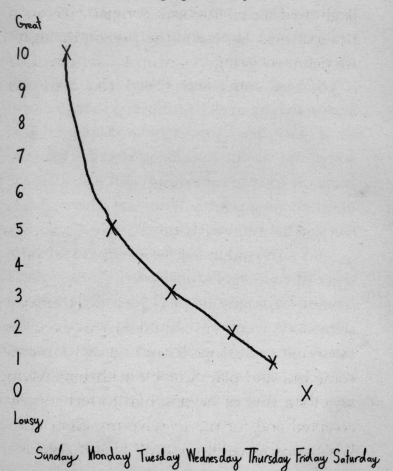

8

Tomorrow can't be worse than today. Nigel told everyone that he came round to my place and met my mum. Now Kirrily says he's my boyfriend. AND I had to say sorry to him this morning or Mum will kill me and Mrs Bright said since I like boys' company so much I can sit next to Nigel. If he nudges me again I'm definitely going to scream. I don't care if he is good at sums and says I can copy his answers.

Friday

Friday is absolute zero on the lousy scale. It's the day we hand in our homework. We had a sheet of times tables to do.

Since I'm grounded I spent all Thursday afternoon in my room. Nigel was hanging around in our lounge room waiting for me to come out and play Scrabble with him. Mum says it's a way of helping him to feel socially accepted and for me to salve my conscience. What conscience? It's not MY fault if Nigel is a dork. I got to the end of my tables sheet for the first time ever. Right up to 12 x 12 = 145. Then Paul sort of waddled in and said "Pooey, Jilly." And he was! I had to open the window wide to get the pong out. When I turned round to take Paul to the bathroom he'd already pulled the nappy off and was trying to wipe his bottom. And guess what he was using.

Mrs Bright won't believe me. She says it's just one of my ingenious excuses for not handing my homework in. It would have been a great excuse if I hadn't done it, but I had. (Must put it in my Secrets Book for future use.) Mrs Bright won't believe me unless I get a note from Mum. Mum's not talking to me because there's baby poo all over my bed. I have to do another tables sheet at recess. Oh, well, Nigel says he'll help me, so I'll get it done in two minutes flat.

Jillian,

Your Journal is interesting and your sentences are well constructed. I'm pleased to see you finally understand line graphs. I must point out that $12 \times 12 = 144$. Write that out twenty times. Next time, do your homework and you'll know your tables. I think your friendship with Nigel is sweet and you are good to help your mother with your baby brother.

Mrs Bright

Monday

Oh heck. I didn't know Mrs Bright was going to collect our journals and read them. I thought we were allowed to write anything we want in them. Even our innermost secrets and private thoughts. Sarah says Mrs Bright wants to find out our secrets because teachers are snoops who give reports about us to our parents. Now when I look at Mrs Bright all I see is a sort of detective like Sherlock Holmes. She reckons she won't be collecting them often and she'll only be glancing at them to see that they're up to date. But Sarah says you can't trust teachers.

I made some more friendship pins on the weekend when I was grounded and I had to look after Paul while the parents were out. This time I didn't use nappy pins. I know now, you have to have little ones. I finally found some holding up the hem of my school tunic, which got ripped when I jumped over the fence. Mum wouldn't fix it because she said I had to, since I did it. Something about consequences. Trouble is, I can't sew.

I used the beads from an old friendship bracelet that Ashley gave me when we used to be best friends, the week before last. (Before she told on me for copying my tables answers off the back of my exercise book. I'm never talking to Ashley again.) There were fifteen beads on it so I put seven on one pin and eight on the other.

This morning I gave them to Kirrily and Skye but they said friendship pins are out.

Everyone's collecting marbles now.

I don't care if I do have to spend all play-time doing my sums again. I must be the only kid in the school who doesn't have marbles.

I'm going to pin up my tunic hem with the friendship pins.

Tuesday

Yesterday afternoon Nigel came round again. Mum let him in. She says he's a good influence because his manners are peckable. He's just a creep. But I couldn't escape because I'm still grounded. So I made him help me with my homework. Richard was cracking up because I can't get division and he kept writing out sums like:

$$Jillian + Nigel = True\ Love$$

$$10 \times Jillian = A\ tonne\ of\ hot\ air.$$

Ha ha ha.

I didn't bash Nigel up. Even though he kept Richard's bits of paper. Nigel's got marbles—a bag full of steelies, but he says they're ball bearings. They're great. He gave me half because I played Scrabble again. I found some excellent words in the dictionary but they're too rude to use in Scrabble so Nigel won again. I made a list of them in my Secrets Book for future use. There are great words in the dictionary.

Nigel is a LYCANTHROPE.

Kirrily is a SYCOPHANT.

Megan can SPONTANEOUSLY combust for all I care.

(If you don't know those words, Mrs B, you know where to look!)

Now I've got a pocket full of steelies but I can't play. I'm not being kept in; I got all my divisions right today. It's just that everybody knows Nigel has steelies, so they'd guess where I got mine from. Playing marbles would ruin what's left of my life.

Wednesday

Mrs Bright has banned marbles. Last year we had a marbles craze which lasted thirteen days before it was banned. This year it was two days. That must be a world record. And it's all Raymond's fault. As usual. If Mrs Bright hadn't caught him selling bonkers to the little kids for fifty cents each during recess yesterday, she wouldn't have been cranky. But she did and then she saw the Third graders digging holes in the grass for their game.

She went mad because we only have a few patches of grass in our playground. It never gets a chance to grow. The big boys play soccer in the middle and the little kids play broom-broom cars and houses around the trees and the middle kids play Batman and war games all round the outside.

(The outside of a shape is called a perimeter. It's like a fence. There's a poster on our classroom wall that says so. I wonder why Mrs Bright covers her posters up when we have a test. They'd be so helpful.)

Mrs Bright yelled at the Third graders and turned away. Her foot went into one of their marble holes and then she fell on her knees onto a pile of marbles.

She should be off the crutches soon. Richard said she over-reacted. Her ankle wasn't broken or anything.

Kirrily is bringing elastics to school tomorrow. I think I will, too.

Thursday

I searched and searched for my elastic but it must have disappeared. The only elastic I could find was in my PJs and undies and I had to tie all the short pieces together but I got a decent sized rope in the end.

This morning when I got to school everyone was hanging around Kirrily. She had this FANTASTIC fluoro green elastic from the shop. Everybody wanted to play with her but she said there were too many kids. So I got my elastic out too and when they saw it they started screaming and laughing. Don't know why, it still stretches. The only kids who wanted to play with me were some Year One kids, who can't even jump, and the Tanger twins who nobody plays with because they smell funny. And Nigel. (I found another word for Nigel: UBIQUITOUS.)

We made the little kids stand at the ends to hold the elastic. I got out straight away. It's hard to jump over elastic when you're trying to hold up your underpants through your tunic.

Friday

Homework day again. This time I got my tables safely to school. AND I got 50/50 for the first time in my life. I got a gold star on the Champs chart. Mrs Bright said Nigel deserved half the star because he's given me so much help. I'm going to look for a suitable word for Mrs Bright tonight. I got 20/20 for my spelling too. Skye was GREEN! (Get it?) Kirrily says I can play elastics with her at lunchtime.

I'm going to ask if I can go to the toilet now. I'm going to try and keep my undies up with sticky tape.

Jillian,

The word is impeccable and I agree with your mother about Nigel. You should try copying Nigel's manners instead of trying to be friends with certain girls.

PS I don't need a dictionary and I don't appreciate those words!

PPS I'm glad you know what a perimeter is because you are going to pick up papers all around the playground perimeter next week. Think pleasant thoughts while you do it. And think about the value of friendships. Nigel will help you, I'm sure.

Mrs Bright

Monday

Mrs Bright limped in this morning and said she was sick of reading about marbles and elastics. (She didn't HAVE to read our journals, did she!) She has given us a topic for five-minute writing. We have to write nonstop for five minutes while she times us with a stopwatch. So here goes.

MY SCHOOL

I don't know what to say about my school. It's just a school. It's called Flora Heights Primary. We have about two hundred children. Mrs Bright says there is an average of twenty-nine children in each grade. I'm in Year Five and we have twenty-five kids so I guess that makes us below average.

In our class there are groups. I call them:

The Princesses—That's Skye, Megan, Kirrily, Sarah and Karlie. And Tegan, too.

The Rough Heads—That's just about all the boys except Nigel. And it includes Amanda.

The Dorks—Nigel. And Vincent. Or is Vincent a Rough Head . . .?

The Normals—The rest of the class, except one or two other kids who are Loners.

I think I must be a Loner. Most of the Normals and Princesses reckon I'm one of the Dorks. Especially since I have to sit next to Nigel. I wish I was a Princess.

Mrs Bright gets really angry when we talk about the groups. She says we're all individuals and we shouldn't label people. I can't help that. It's tradition.

Tuesday

MY SCHOOL (for five more minutes)

Our school is sort of in the country. Flora Heights is 2km away and we're surrounded by paddocks with cows in them. Mrs Bright says we're bovine too. I thought that meant country kids until I looked it up in the dictionary. Ha, ha. We get to school by bus or we ride bikes. Some get driven. The bike kids are luckiest because they get to school first and get the best equipment to play with.

I get the bus. The Rough Heads sit up the back of the bus and do leans when the bus goes round the corners. If you're on the end you get squashed. I love that game but Raymond won't let me sit at the back any more. He says I've been Nigellated.

The Princesses sit in the middle and talk about Grade Six boys and popstars and hair and things. Except Kirrily. She gets a ride in her mum's car. She gives her best friend a lift home. She chooses a different best friend each day. I haven't ever been her best friend.

The little kids and the goody-goodies sit at the front so Jack (he's the driver) can make them feel safe. And Brett HAS to sit at the very front so he can't light matches or draw rude pictures on the seats.

I sit wherever I can find a seat. There's always a space next to Nigel. Worst luck.

Wednesday

MY SCHOOL (for five MORE minutes)

We've got seven teachers and a principal and a library teacher and a release teacher. That's too many teachers. There's a school secretary and a cleaner and a man who cuts the grass.

The principal is Mr Bigg. Good name for a principal. Mr Connors teaches Year Six. I'm dead scared of going to his class because he LOVES maths. He teaches it all the time. Except when he's giving lectures. Some of the big boys have stopwatches and time him when he gets started on a Serious Topic. His world record is 1 hour, 46 minutes and 53 seconds talking about Attitude Being A Little Thing That Makes A Big Difference. Some of the kids in his class do their maths while he's lecturing. Some pass notes. Marty goes to sleep. You always know the lecture is over when Mr Connors starts yelling at Marty. Poor Marty. He sits up half the night playing Spiders of Doom on his computer. He needs his sleep in class.

We think our teachers are holding a shouting competition. So far Mr Connors is ahead for yelling the loudest. But NO-ONE can beat Mrs Bright for the sudden unexpected explosion. But anyone would yell if they had Raymond. His mum sure does.

Thursday

MY SCHOOL (yet another five minutes)

Writing about school is boring, boring, boring. And I like writing. It's one thing I CAN do. I can read pretty well too. And lately my spelling has improved. Mrs Bright told Mum I have an advanced vocabulary and Mum grounded me because she thought I must be using inappropriate words at school.

We do lots of writing and language. Mrs Bright says the more we practise the better we'll be at it.

Some of the kids hate writing. That's because the only writing they do is on the walls of the toilets. Sam got in mega trouble yesterday. His five minute writing went like this:

i hax shcool it sux

I don't like it when Sam gets in trouble. His mum left home and he can't get into his house until his dad gets home real late. He's got no-one to help him with his homework and he's even worse at maths than me.

I'm not playing elastics anymore. Kirrily said I can't because I'm Nigellated. I hate Kirrily. Maybe I'll sit with Sam at playtime and help him do his homework. At least he'll get some of his tables right.

Friday

Yesterday Sam came round to my place and hung around the back door. Mum asked him in but he wouldn't come. So I went out and we went to the tree house. Sam had his homework crumpled up in his pocket. We did our homework and then Sam showed me how to make a slingshot.

We hid in the tree house and took shots at kids going past. Sam hit Richard and I got Nigel. Bullseye. But I didn't feel glad for long. Nigel's face sort of screwed up as he ran off. The way your face goes when you're hurt and trying not to cry. My face went the same way when I saw Nigel like that. I gave the slingshot to Sam.

Jillian,
    Thank you for helping Sam. How do you intend making it up to Nigel? Dork is an inappropriate word.
    Mrs Bright

Monday

ROLE MODELS

We had to talk about role models this morning. A role model is someone who has qualities you admire and copy so you can be a better person. Mrs Bright made a list of our suggestions for role models. There were lots of cricketers and footballers. Some of the kids said rock singers and supermodels because they earn lots of money. Mrs Bright wasn't impressed. But she really got mad when Raymond repeated my suggestion for him out loud. She told him he has to research and find out if Genghis Khan IS actually an appropriate role model.

Thanks a lot, Raymond. Now we ALL have to do research and find a famous person to be our personal role model. We have to do projects on them. Juliet says she's doing Florence Nightingale and Megan's doing her dad's hero, a lady called Mrs Thatcher. I don't know who to pick. My mum isn't famous.

Tuesday

Yesterday I went to the town library to look up role models. I asked the librarian to show me where to look. She said to wait a minute, she'd get me a helper. Guess who? Nigel. He says he's her friend. He hangs around the library when he's not at my place. The librarian said that the library is like Nigel's second home, he's there so much. She didn't seem all that thrilled when she said it though.

Anyway Nigel took me to a section labelled BIOGRAPHY. (Mrs Bright, a biography is a life story. An AUTObiography is your life story written by yourself. Does a journal count as an autobiography?)

Nigel showed off like he owns the library. He's such a PAIN. I pretended I didn't know him after he showed me where the books were. But he started to act normal so we ended up looking through the books together.

We found a perfect role model for Marty. Someone who:

Sleeps all day
Is active at night
Is a parasite
Never works.
Can you guess, Mrs Bright?

(It's Dracula)

Wednesday

Nigel, Sam and I started looking in books for our own role models yesterday. But first we looked up Genghis Khan to see how much he's like Raymond. Well, if Ray grows up to be like this Genghis we're in big trouble. He conquered the Mongols, overran China and invaded India. His empire stretched from the Yellow Sea to the Black Sea. He's famous for being extra cruel.

We started a list of possibles. Then we started matching famous people to people we know.

We decided that Nigel should have Melvil Dewey because they both love libraries.

Kirrily or Skye could have Shirley Temple.

In fact ALL the Princesses could have her.

Raymond could have Billy the Kid (an outlaw who first killed a man at age twelve!) Better than Genghis, at least.

Nigel said Richard should have Albert Einstein.

I said Sam should take Alexander the Great. He was a really little man who conquered heaps of places. Sam might learn to be a winner, too.

Then we started finding role models for the teachers. Mr Bigg could have Atilla the Hun. But we couldn't decide for Mrs Bright. The boys wanted Queen Elizabeth 1 because she ruled EVERYONE, males included. But I wanted Queen Boadicea, who ruled these people called Iceni in Britain when the Romans invaded. She painted herself blue and charged off to fight the invaders.

We laughed so much at the idea of Mrs Bright painted blue and swinging a sword at Raymond that the librarian threw us out. Nigel won't talk to me, ever again. Isn't that a good thing? So why do I feel all sick inside?

Thursday

I don't know what to write and I don't know who to choose for a role model. Mrs Boadicea is charging around the room like she's looking for some Romans to kill.

I want to go home.

Friday

Last night I couldn't go to the library. Mum says I have to stop being a mischief maker who gets nice little boys like Nigel into trouble. I said that Nigel can get himself into trouble without any help from me, so I got sent to my room. I did my homework. Pity I forgot to put it in my bag.

Then I had nothing to do so I sneaked into Richard's room and pulled a book from his shelves. It's called FRANKENSTEIN.

Jillian,

I'm not sure whether I'm insulted or flattered about the comparisons to Elizabeth I and Boadicea. But even flattery will not make me believe fairy stories about homework left at home. I was a child once, you know!

Queen B

Monday

Mrs Bright said she was only going to collect and read these journals occasionally. But she's been collecting them every Friday, then having a good old read over the weekend and handing them back on Monday morning. Sarah was right—you can't trust teachers. I asked Mrs Bright if "occasionally" in teacher-speak meant "regularly" and she put me on time-out for impertinence. I'll have to look that one up but I think I know what it will mean. Cheeky.

I read ALL weekend. *Frankenstein* is really

scary. It's about a man who creates a monster-man and it all goes wrong. You end up not really sure which is the monster—the scientist or his creation. It's sad and it's frightening. Richard says I should be in a movie called *Bride of Frankenstein*. Sure. Even I know that Frankenstein is the scientist, not the monster. So: ha, ha, Richard.

I'm never getting married. All boys are Frankenstein monsters.

Tuesday

YAY! I've finally got my role model. I found out that *Frankenstein* was written by a woman. A YOUNG woman. Mary Wollstonecraft Shelley. She started writing the book as a game with friends who were all telling scary stories.

I want to write books which will be so famous that in a hundred years' time everyone will know my characters. Nigel can keep his Dewey Decimal System.

Wednesday

Mrs Bright asked everyone who their role models are. She loves Nigel's choice, of course. She didn't love the Princesses' choices. They all chose different members of this all-girl singing group who starve themselves, and their singing sounds like the cats outside at night. When I told her about Mary Shelley, Mrs Bright just went "Hmmmmm".

Nigel still hates me. He told everyone what *Frankenstein* is about, from movies he's seen. Now they're calling me Bride of Frankenstein and asking me if I screwed my head bolts in properly today. Duhh. Raymond drew a picture of me and passed it round. This is it.

Jilan Franknstn

Raymond should learn to spell while he's on detention. Mrs Bright says he hasn't got a future in Art.

Thursday

I'm writing this on time-out. Kirrily told Mrs Bright that I was reading while we were supposed to be doing Journals. Mrs Bright checked all my work and found I haven't done any maths this week. I wish I was Doctor Frankenstein. I'd set my monster onto Kirrily. Then Nigel. And Raymond. And then . . . look out, Mrs Bright!

Friday

Time-out again. This time it's for thumping Raymond. I asked the teacher why Raymond isn't on time-out as well for stomping around me making monster noises. Mr Bigg says there is no excuse for violent behaviour, and I must have a bad attitude if I can't take a little innocent fun or cope with minor frustration.

At least I can read my book in peace now. After I finish this week's maths.

Jillian,
    I appreciate your ambition to become an author like Mary Shelley, but please refrain from threatening violence. It's no wonder Nigel has been avoiding you. And no matter what your classmates say, you can trust teachers!
    Mrs Bright

Monday

Mrs Bright has been reading us a book called *Billy and the Genie*. It's about this boy who finds an old bottle on the beach and when he opens it a genie pops out and gives him three wishes. But the wishes unexpectedly go wrong, no matter how carefully the boy asks for them.

Billy asked for his maths test to be all correct and it worked. But the teacher called his parents and told them Billy was cheating. And no-one believed him about the genie, so he was in big trouble. Makes you think, though. If I had a genie, I'd ask it to create a Frankenstein's monster. Goodbye, Raymond.

Tuesday

Mum has a saying: "Great minds think alike". Mrs Bright must have a great mind like mine. Today after we listened to *Billy and the Genie* we had a discussion about genies and what we would wish for. (I did NOT mention my Monster, Mrs Bright, because my latest dictionary word is discretion.) Most of the kids said they'd wish for a never-ending supply of wishes, or for their own personal video-game arcades.

Then Mrs Bright went and spoiled it all by saying we had to write a story about what we would wish for if we had three wishes. The wishes had to backfire. That's her way of saying they went wrong.

Wednesday

Nigel spent all morning helping Sam with his story. Sam says the words, Nigel writes them down. Nigel got an early mark at recess.

I don't care. I'm writing a FANTASTIC story about this monster who is actually a genie and has a kind heart and helps me when people are mean to me. His kind heart is hurt when people make fun of me because I'm not a Princess. So far he's turned Richard into a calculator and Nigellated Nigel. He's going to turn Mrs Bright into a sunbeam next. (Get it? Bright—sunbeam.)

Thursday

We published our stories today and read them out. Skye's story was pathetic. She wished to have even more beautiful, long, blonde, curly hair, so the genie made her into a supermodel instead of a kid. Then she wished to be mega-rich, so the genie turned her into that Bill guy who invented personal computers. Then she wished to be taller and slimmer and the genie turned her into a telegraph pole. Mrs Bright loved it. Skye thinks she'll be an author now.

Friday

Sam read his story out to the class today. He's really improved in his reading and this is the best story he's written. It was the first time he's volunteered to read out loud. It's probably the last time too. Everyone laughed at him because he got the idea of backfiring wrong. His story went something like this.

"I wished for a new car and drove it. But it backfired. So I wished I had a new motorbike to drive to the shop but it backfired. Then I wished for a new baby brother but he backfired."

When the others started guessing how a baby can backfire, Sam had a fit and ran out of the school. Mrs Bright is SO MAD at everyone! I am, too. I hope I can find Sam this afternoon.

Jillian,
    Great minds DO think alike. We think alike about Sam.
        Mrs Bright (Sunbeam)

Monday

Nigel came round on Friday and we went looking for Sam. We searched around Sam's yard and round the school grounds. We rode our bikes around the streets. We even went to the town library but I stayed outside while Nigel went in to look. Then we went down to the quarry but Raymond threw rocks at us. Just as well we had our crash hats on. Raymond has a killer aim. I'm in trouble because my crash hat is dented. Sam wasn't there either.

We rode back to my place because Nigel said if I wrote a letter of apology to the librarian we could be friends again. I want to see if Mary Shelley wrote anything else, so I agreed. When we got home Sam was in our tree house. We dragged him inside, and Mum let him stay for tea and said he could sleep over on the lounge.

Tuesday

I hate sport. I hate it. I hate it. I loathe and detest sport. We had to play T-Ball yesterday. Skye and Raymond were captains. Skye gets to be captain because she's a goody-goody and the teacher says she's got leadership qualities. Raymond gets chosen because he won't cooperate if anyone else is in charge. I don't think tripping up the other team's players and hitting your own when they get out is cooperating. But it's better than Raymond climbing into the trees and pelting us with gumnuts until Mr Bigg gets him down.

I told Mrs Bright that I was really sick and

couldn't play. She said I had to play unless I was dying. Then I asked if I could be excused from T-Ball to do my divisions and she said I was a malingerer.

I'm looking that word up tonight.

Wednesday

Thankyou very much, Mrs Bright. I found a word too. You MALIGN me. I found that when I was looking for MALINGERER. And now I am going to CONTRADICT something you say.

Sport is NOT a healthy activity.

First, just think what it does to my self-esteem to stand there while every other kid gets chosen by Skye and Raymond, one by one, until there's only me and Nigel left. Then Nigel gets chosen by Ray because at least he's a boy and won't spread girl germs. Then Skye sulks because she was FORCED to have me.

Second, think how my self-esteem suffers when I have to sit on the end of the team and be ignored by the Princesses.

Third, what does it do for my mental health to sit there, bored and suffering when I could be reading? Not to mention my hearing, when I get screamed at because I didn't hear you yell "Batter up".

And Fourth, can you imagine how humiliating it is to walk up, knowing you're going to miss and have to run, knowing you're going to trip over or get caught out? Knowing you're going to go back to be screamed at by your teammates and laughed at by the others. Or thumped by Raymond.

Sport is HAZARDOUS to the health.

Thursday

I have to go straight home today to wash my sports clothes. Mum says if I insist on crawling through mud and rolling on the grass, I can clean up the consequences.

Mary Shelley did not write *Bride of Frankenstein*. Or *Dracula*.

Friday

Mrs Bright, why did I only get a B for my genie story? It's the best one I ever wrote. And I checked the spelling and punctuation. And my descriptions were very descriptive.

Jillian,

Your story was well written and imaginative. Your spelling is remarkable. The reason you did not receive an A is because your story was vindictive. The backfiring of the wishes was supposed to happen to the wisher; you made the victims of your wishes suffer. A wish for someone to have a toothache should not result in the loss of twenty-eight teeth!

Mrs Bright

PS Thank you for looking after Sam and for being a friend to Nigel again.

Monday

I LOVE writing. We're writing poetry. Mrs Bright says we have to do acrostics first. They're easy. But we aren't allowed to do our own name. We have to pull someone else's name out of a hat and do an acrostic about them. I got Skye. Nigel got me. Raymond got Sam. Sam got Juliet. I can't wait to hear them.

HAPPY

Huffing and puffing with anticipation
Acrostics are
Perfect ways of showing
Personality.
Yay!

Tuesday

Now we're ALL on detention. Mrs Bright went ballistic when we read out our drafts. Why do I always get the blame? She said my vindictive attitude is affecting everyone. I asked her, if my attitudes are so influential to others, doesn't that mean I have leadership qualities? So now I've got double detention for cheek. I read out my acrostic first. I thought it was pretty good because it showed Skye's personality.

<u>SKYE</u>

Spitefully sweet,
Killer caterwauler,
You REALLY think you'll
Ever become a mega popstar?

Skye started crying. Then Raymond read his.

<u>SAM</u>

Sam is
A
Moron.

Sam started crying. He tried to run away but Mrs Bright had hold of him.

Sam's acrostic:

JULIET

Jumping
Up and down
Like an
Insect
Every
Tuesday.

Juliet started crying because everyone started buzzing and hopping around her. Now she knows what it feels like. But I suppose that's a vindictive thought.

Wednesday

I'm NEVER going to speak to Nigel again. Ever, ever. He reckoned it was a compliment.

JILLIAN

Jolly and jocular, jocund and jiggly,
Into writing and reading, but not T-Ball,
Loving her friends, like Sam and Me,
Loathing Skye, her worst enemy,
I
Am going to marry her. Her
Name will be mine: Quigley.

I can NEVER show my face in public again. I've begged Mrs Bright to put me on permanent time-out. But she said Nigel's acrostic was adorable and well-meant and that I have to learn not to be so passionate about Life's Slings and Arrows. Whatever that means. I wish I was dead.

Thursday

Went straight home yesterday and shut myself in my room. I had a headache from where I fell against a pole in the bus because I had to pull my beanie down over my face so I couldn't see everyone grinning at me. I could still hear them singing "Here comes the Bride, all jiggly and wide."

Mum came in when I didn't go down for tea. I told her about the acrostics and Frankenstein and being Nigellated and slings and arrows and wanting to be dead. She cried. I cried. Richard came in but went out when he saw Mum crying. His face looked funny but I couldn't laugh.

Mum told me about slings and arrows. There was this man called Hamlet who couldn't make his mind up what to do and went around talking to himself about it. Mum showed me the play where he's trying to decide whether to go to sleep or fight everyone or just put up with it all. He says:

> To be, or not to be: that is the question:
> Whether 'tis nobler in the mind to suffer
> The slings and arrows of outrageous fortune,
> Or to take arms against a sea of troubles,
> And by opposing end them.

I think that means I put up with the hurts
and pains of life or fight everybody who
upsets me. Mum says I can't fight everyone
who offends me because we all have problems
and we can't be at war all the time. She says I
should just suffer the slings and arrows of
outrageous Nigel, and consider what he might
be suffering in his own life. I felt better after
that. I'm going to tell Sam about slings and
arrows too. But I'm still never talking to Nigel.

Friday

We all had to write new acrostics today. Nice
ones. This is Karlie's acrostic about Sarah:

SARAH

Sarah, Sarah, so sweet.
Are you my best friend?
Really, you're my best friend,
Always.
Heaven sent.

Puke. I had to write a nice one about Skye. I got writer's block. I'm on detention until I do it. I don't care. Detention is a Nigel-free zone.

Jillian,
   I am sorry you feel so stressed about your life. But your mother is right. You must learn to make allowances for the feelings and needs of other people. You isolate yourself by your refusal to compromise.

   Mrs Bright

Monday

Only one week till the holidays. I feel like Hamlet. I can't make up my mind if I want holidays or school. Which could be worse? Two weeks of Richard and Paul? Or two weeks of Kirrily and Company. (That's their new pop group name. They practise at recess on the concrete. The little kids hang around and cheer.

The big boys hang around and laugh and call out rude comments.)

I go down to the bottom playground and collect seed pods. The pods of the silkyoaks are perfect for making little birds. You put cottonwool into the open part and dab on red marker pen, and you've got a robin.

Seedpod
stem makes beak

Curly bit makes tail

Cotton wool with
marker pen

Tuesday

During the holidays I will do these things:
1. Avoid anybody called Richard, Nigel, Kirrily or Skye.
2. Keep the radio turned off so I don't hear any girl singing groups.

3. Make a big picture of a tree with a flock of seedpod birds in the branches. I'll use bark and sticks for the tree.
4. Try AGAIN to teach Paul to use the potty.
5. Read books by lady writers.
6. Read biographies about lady writers.
7. Write a book of acrostics about everyone I know.

(Don't worry, Mrs Bright, I won't publish them. And I won't be VINDICTIVE. Just truthful.)

Wednesday

Three days to go. I can't play today. Yesterday in sport I got stuck on Raymond's team because he got last choice. I actually hit the ball and made it to third base, but while I was waiting to run home I saw some excellent seed pods and started collecting them. I got caught out. Raymond was angry. Now my shins are bruised an interesting purple colour.

But Raymond is on detention too, for violence. I asked Mrs Bright to put me into solitary confinement for my own protection.

Thursday

My bruises are starting to go brown and green. Not pretty. I have added Raymond to my list of people to avoid in the holidays. He doesn't know the meaning of the word VENDETTA, but he does know STALKER and PAYBACK. Maybe school is safer. At least the teachers offer some protection. One more day.

Friday

Last day. It's a Mufti day. You come out of uniform and pay a gold coin as a fine. The money goes to a Worthy Cause.

The Princesses have planned what they're wearing for weeks. They're all wearing shiny sleeveless tops with silver butterflies on the front, and tiny little skirts, and strappy sandals with high heels. They've got clips in their hair, which have butterflies with waggly wings. Skye must have about a hundred in her hair. Kirrily is sulking because she hasn't got as many. She says Skye broke the rules by wearing more than everyone else.

I'm wearing my jeans and joggers and the only jumper I could find. Gran knitted it. It used to be Richard's and it's got the Fat Controller from Thomas the Tank Engine on the front. Mrs Bright says it's cute and the Fat Controller would be a better role model for me than an old monster.

Why do I even bother? But who cares. I'm warm. Today's the last day. And all the Princesses are freezing in their little tops and skirts.

Term Two

55

Monday

A REPORT ON MY HOLIDAYS

The Best Thing: the best thing about my holiday was the ABSENCES. No Juliet, no Kirrily, no Skye and not a sign of Nigel or Raymond. And Richard went to a maths camp!!!

The Worst Thing: Paul. He found my almost-finished bird picture and squashed every seed pod bird with his fist. Mum had no sympathy because I was supposed to be keeping an eye on him at the time.

A Success: Sam read a whole book. He read a chapter out loud to me each day. So I gave him lunch each day. He's stoked. Mum says I'm learning to be kind.

A Disaster: Paul. He refuses to be toilet trained. He screamed "No potty! No potty!" Every time I took off his nappy he ran away and hid somewhere. I'm still finding nasty little clues about his hiding places.

How My Holiday Could Have Been

Improved: a declaration of a Brother-free Zone. Why can't we take our holidays when it suits us, at different times? I'd love to have my mum to myself.

How I Feel About Being Back: mixed. I won't miss nappies. On the other hand, Paul's screaming is better than Kirrily's singing.

My Goal For This Term: TO SURVIVE.

Tuesday

MY GOAL FOR THIS TERM

I thought that TO SURVIVE summed it up perfectly. But noooo. Mrs Bright wants more. So my goal for this term is: to be friendly to everyone no matter how much I hate them, so I can be socially acceptable at school.

Wednesday

My goal was doomed from the start. This term the craze is pets. Everyone is boasting about their pets and forming new groups.

There is The Cat Club. The girls who have cats are in it but they won't let me in because my cat is only a moggie. They say only pedigree cats are allowed. I think the real reason they won't let me in is because I asked them if the club name describes the animals or the owners.

There is The Dog Boys. You have to be a boy, as well as have a dog. And they won't let in little yappy dogs. I suppose that's an insult to me.

Raymond has The Reptile Guys. Half of them don't have a pet, but you're in if Raymond says so. And they all used to collect lizards when they were little. It's safer if you're in Raymond's group but he won't let me in even if I do have three terrapins. He says terrapins are amphibians because they swim. I say they're reptiles but I can't go to Nigel territory to borrow a book to prove it. I have ignored Nigel's existence for three weeks.

I guess I'm a loner again. No-one else has hermit crabs.

Thursday

The Cat Club clusters under the sun shelter. The Dog Boys dally around the Tree. The Reptile Guys crawl along the fence. I shelter in a hole I made under the bushes in the bottom playground. Like a hermit crab in a shell. I can think there. Today Nigel oozed in too. Then Sam crawled in. The Reptile Guys were hunting amphibians to eat. They said Nigel is a toad and Sam is a tadpole. I could hardly throw Nigel out to that treatment so we all lurked together.

Sam told Nigel about his reading. Nigel told us that he didn't see a single kid from our class all holidays. He spent the holiday at the library. He said he was hoping we'd come in, but we never did. The librarian has forgiven me.

Friday

Reptiles on the Rampage.
Dogs Destroying Disgustingly.
Cats Caterwauling on the Concrete.

I LOVE alliteration. But I've gone off lizards.

We had to write alliteration sentences today. They make a sort of poem. I thought Mrs Bright had gone off poetry since we did those acrostics.

I'm doing an alliteration sentence for every letter of the alphabet. I'm up to C. This is my draft:

Crabs Crawling Cautiously a
Cross Kelp from one
Crustacean Carapace to Continue
their Crabby Continuum.

Daggy Dogs will be the subject of letter D. Mrs Bright, names WILL be named for letters S, R, N and K, so they probably won't be published.

Jillian

I was so thrilled to hear Sam's reading this week. You are being a true friend to him. I am glad that you have resolved your differences with Nigel too. Your alliterative sentences are stupendously splendid and sibilantly slick.

Mrs Bright

Monday

Richard found my alliteration sentence notebook on Saturday. He took it to the tree house and shouted the insulting ones out to the whole street. Then he made the pages into paper aeroplanes and flew them in all directions. Vincent picked up the one about Raymond and gave it to him.

Raymond appears to be offended. He doesn't even know half the words but any excuse will do to thump me.

I don't think that: *Rampaging Raymond Riots*

Roughly and Rips aRound Rattily wRiting Rudely is offensive to someone like Raymond, but he sat on our front fence all weekend, staring at the windows. I stayed inside and looked after Paul.

Tuesday

Yesterday Raymond was waiting at the gate at home time. He followed me on to the bus and sat next to me instead of going to the back to play leans. I was dead scared all the way. I kept thinking of those people who carry knives. But he got off at his stop, the one before mine, and I was still alive. When I was able to breathe again and look around, I saw a folded paper on the seat beside me. It had *Jilan Jams* written on it. I'd know that spelling anywhere. I grabbed Raymond's note and shoved it under my jumper before anyone else could see it. I haven't read it. I'm too scared to read death threats.

Last night I dreamed about being pelted with gigantic gumnuts and tripped over cliff tops.

Wednesday

Raymond got on the bus this morning and sat next to me again. He stared at me all the way to school. I could see him in the reflection on the window. He had a funny smile, like he enjoyed seeing me dead scared. I think I'm being stalked.

I'm going to get my maths all wrong today so I can stay in at lunch and do it again. I'm very, very nervous. My life is like a horror movie and I'm never going to write another word about anyone.

Thursday

Yesterday I stayed back and helped Mrs Bright pin up our paintings. Then I washed the brushes and sorted them into wides and fine points. Then she made me leave.

I'd missed the bus so I started walking. But I wasn't safe after all. Raymond was lurking at the next bus stop and stood up when he saw me. I walked quicker and he followed me. I ran. He ran. I ran into the library and hid in the reference section but he didn't follow me in. He's never been inside a library in his whole life. Nigel found me crouching there and he walked me home. I don't suppose he'd be much protection, but Raymond had disappeared.

Friday

I didn't want to come to school today. I lay in bed with my head under the covers and groaned and held my breath until I was hot and puffed. Mum said it was obviously homework day and dragged me out by the foot. I was so scared about Raymond I started crying and even Mum knows I only cry about serious things. Not homework. No offence, Mrs Bright. But I like doing homework now. Mostly.

Mum dragged the story out of me. I told her it was the worst sling or arrow of outrageous fortune ever hurled at me.

She made me get the note and we opened it. It said:

Jilan jigles lik jelly when she jumps on Julet, will you be my frend. Rampaging Ray.

I was so relieved it wasn't a death threat I cried. Then I was so horrified that Raymond was asking to be my friend that I cried even more. That would make me a girl Reptile Guy. A Reptile Chick. A girl Rough Head. Like Amanda. I'd have to play Hunt the Amphibian. But Amanda never gets thumped. She also never gets into the other girls' games.

Mum drove me to school because I missed the bus. I felt like a Princess.

Jillian

You must know you can come and talk with me when you're troubled. I hope you've learnt a lesson about writing vindictive comments about your classmates.

Mrs Bright

Monday

I can't do it.

I worried all weekend. In the end, Richard came up with a good idea. He said that if I have a dilemma I should make a list of the pros and cons and make a decision. After I looked up dilemma in the dictionary I started.

WHETHER TO BE RAYMOND'S FRIEND.

PROS (Reasons for)	CONS (Reasons against)
1. He'll stop thumping me.	1. He'll be meaner to me.
2. He might be nice to Sam and Nigel.	2. He might scare Sam and Nigel off.
3. Mrs B. will be pleased.	3. Mrs B. might be cross.
4. I'll have someone to talk to.	4. I'll be a Rough Head.
5. I can sit at the back of the bus.	5. I might start swearing.
6. Kirrily and Skye won't dare call me a dork.	6. I'll never get to be a Princess.
7. Nigel might leave me alone.	7. Nigel might stop helping me.
8. Ray might bash up Richard.	8. Richard might get hurt.
9. Any friend is better than none.	9. Raymond hates everyone else.
10. I'd be protected from slings and arrows.	10. I might cop more slings and arrows.

Both sides were evenly balanced. Every pro had a con. So I worried. Then I fell asleep and dreamed. In my dream I got married to Raymond and no-one else would speak to me. Ray pelted gumnuts at people who went past our house.

I just can't do it. I'll have to tell Raymond NO on the bus this arvo.

Tuesday

Raymond CRIED. He went all red and water came out of his eyes and nose. He had to rub his face with his sleeve. He was making a sort of hiccupping snorting noise which hurt me inside. I cried. Nigel saw me crying and he started crying. Sam cried too. I think he was scared of what Raymond would do when he stopped crying. We huddled together so the others couldn't see we were crying.

I got off the bus and ran home to Mum. She read my dilemma sheet and listened to my decision.

Then she let me lie on the lounge with my head on her lap.

Then she ordered takeaway pizza for tea. This must be serious.

At bedtime she told me to sleep and not worry because things have a way of working themselves out. I slept like a log.

When I got up, Mum looked as if she'd been awake all night worrying. But that's silly. She couldn't have. She told ME not to worry.

Wednesday

Today I deliberately got all my work wrong so I could be on time-out to do corrections. But my plan backfired. Mrs Bright kept me in, all right. But she wanted to talk to me. She wanted to know if I needed to talk to her about any problem I might have at home or school.

How could I tell her I had boy problems with Raymond?

So I lied. I'm sorry, Mrs Bright.

I told her that I was tired because Richard keeps the TV on loud really late watching football. She sent me to the reading corner to have a rest. I hope she doesn't tell Mum. Mum would kill me if she knew I fibbed about Richard.

Thursday

At home time yesterday I hung around trying to help Mrs Bright until the bus was gone. When she forced me out, the coast was clear. No bus, only Mum's car! I ran over and jumped in the front. But in the back was Sam. And Nigel. And Raymond.

Mum said she'd invited my little friends to come over for afternoon tea while she was waiting for me.

When we got home she gave us milkshakes and cake in the tree house. Richard and Paul weren't outside so it was just us four. I couldn't speak. Nigel was silent and sort of trembling. Sam ate. Raymond just stared at me while he was eating. I don't think it was a stalker stare though. More like a big dog when it wants you to pat it.

Then he said, "Your mum's cool." I said, "Yeah." So did Nigel and Sam. Well, Sam went "Mmmfffh" through his cake.

We went inside and watched TV until Mum told us to do our homework. After that the others went home. Nigel said thanks for having us to Mum, and Sam and Raymond said it after him. Mum says my friends are nice little boys.

I didn't know whether to laugh or cry. So I hugged Mum and thumped Richard.

Friday

Today in school Nigel, Sam, Raymond and I all got a gold star for tables. Everybody clapped Sam and Raymond. It's the first time they've ever got a star. Sam was grinning like his face would split. Raymond looked really angry and his face went all red. But he folded the tables sheet up carefully and put it in his pocket. Mrs Bright's eyes went all watery.

At recess, I was going down to the bottom playground when Raymond grabbed me and pulled me behind the big bush. He sort of growled, "I do want to be your friend. I never had one before."

So I said, "Well, OK. But there are conditions. Like, you've got to put up with Sam and Nigel. And you've got to stop hitting me."

He said, "I wouldn't do nothink to make your mum mad. Ummm . . . has she got more cake?" Then he sort of grinned.

We're all going to play Spotlight on the weekend.

Jillian,
    I am glad you caught up with your sleep!
    Seriously, though, I am glad your mother was able to help you. Remember, I'm here at school to help you too. Trust me.
    Mrs Bright

Monday

All weekend Sam, Ray, Nigel and I hung around together. We went down to the quarry with our bikes and Ray showed us how to do jumps.

When Vincent came and yelled that we were all Nigellated, Raymond grabbed him by the shirt. He was going to thump him but he looked at me. Sam and Nigel and I all yelled together "Don't do it Ray!" We don't like Vincent. We just know what Ray's thumpings feel like. Ray let him drop and Vincent was so shocked he said, "Sorry." Then we let Vincent play too.

On Sunday we made the tree house into a fortress. No-one can enter unless they know the secret password, or we let them in. We might let Richard in if he shows us about those co-ordinate things in maths.

Tuesday

Yesterday Mrs Bright declared our room a No Put-Down Zone.

A put-down is making someone feel bad by your actions or looks or words. I whispered to Nigel that our whole school is a frontline active put-down War Zone. He started to giggle that stupid giggle of his and Mrs Bright told him to stop laughing like a kookaburra. Raymond yelled out that that was a put-down to kookaburras. Then Mrs Bright said Raymond was putting Nigel down.

I wanted to ask if a joke between friends is a put-down. I also wanted to ask if a teacher's comment about a kid's laugh is a put-down, but I didn't dare. I actually WANT to go out to play today. Raymond's showing Nigel and me how to kick a soccer ball.

Wednesday

Having a No Put-Down Zone in our room is making conversation very difficult.

Kirrily showed her collection of hairbands for News. Then she asked, "Do you like them?" The Princesses all said yes but you could tell they were all so jealous they wished her butterfly clips would fly away. The rest of us couldn't say yes. We despise hair decorations. And we couldn't say no because we'd be accused of being nasty. So we did the only thing possible and said nothing. Kirrily started crying and Mrs Bright went mad at us for putting Kirrily down by our refusal to interact.

Then Rodney talked about football. He's new and he wants the other boys to like him so he's memorized all the rules and statistics about Rugby League and soccer and Rugby Union and Aussie Rules and even Irish Football, only he calls it Garlic Football. He told us the scores for every game last weekend and the teams' places on the Competition Ladder and how many tries each player has scored in his career and lots more I can't remember.

Megan likes Rodney. She said his talk was fascinating. Skye asked him what colour costumes each team's cheerleaders wear. Then Mrs Bright asked me what I thought. At the time I was writing a list in my Secrets Book of SYNONYMS FOR BORING so she caught me by surprise.

I said "Oh, Rodney was err . . . very . . . err . . . interesting. What was he talking about again?"

Now I'll miss my kicking lesson at lunchtime. I have to write out "Ignoring my classmate's news is a put-down" fifty times. In running writing.

What Mrs Bright doesn't realise is Rodney has probably never touched a rugby ball in his life. Plump boys with well-brushed hair and calculators in their shirt pockets don't generally play contact sports.

But I guess that's not her point. Respecting my classmate's interests IS. Even if their interest is fantasy. Even if they don't respect MY interests in return.

Thursday

Kirrily and Skye and Megan have made a club. They call it the NPDs. That means No Put-Downers. Mrs Bright thinks it's sweet and lets them sit together at the front near her desk. They're going to let Rodney join. When they finish their work they go round and help other kids.

Skye decided to help Sam today. He gets stuck on these maths grid things where you have to find the rule and fill in the missing numbers. Skye patted him on the head and said, "You're doing REALLY well, Sam. You might even get some right one day!" Sam socked her in the face and ran out. Skye cried and blubbed that she was only trying to help. Mrs Bright talked to Skye for ages in the corner but Skye kept sniffling and going on about trying to help less fortunate people.

I asked Mrs Bright if I could go after Sam but she wouldn't let me. I said that pretending to be nice to Sam when his work was all wrong is a put-down. Mrs Bright said I was suffering from the Green-eyed Monster and must learn to share my friends.

What do you mean, Mrs Bright? Skye hasn't got green eyes, they're brown. (You're right about the monster bit. But isn't that a put-down?)

Friday

Every Friday Richard goes off to school yelling "TGIF!" I had to give him my recess cake for three Fridays before he told me it means Thank Goodness It's Friday. Now we both go off yelling "TGIF!"

This has been one of the worst weeks ever. Mrs Bright keeps going on about put-downs and giving me grim looks. So Skye and Kirrily give me dirty looks too. They asked Mrs Bright if they could change their seats to be near Rodney, to support him. So I asked Mrs Bright if I could move near to Nigel and Raymond and Sam and support them. Mrs Bright called me a Mischief Maker.

Now she says our room is being ruined by Little Exclusive Groups and she intends to Do Something About It.

If I really thought she was talking about the Cat Girls and the Rodney group I would agree with her. But somehow I think she means me and the boys.

Jillian,

I've told you before but I'll say it once more: you must learn to consider others. Rodney is still upset about the way you ignored his news. He thought you were insulting him. He needs support.

Mrs Bright

Monday

I was in the tree house on Saturday talking with the boys about school. We were wondering what Mrs Bright was planning. Nigel said that if he was the teacher he would ban clubs. Raymond said he'd ban girls. I said I would ban all mention of popstars and hairdressing. Sam said he wished that he could make school like a party he went to once, before his mum disappeared. Everyone played games together, and there was a clown in charge and everyone was laughing.

IT HIT ME WITH A BLINDING FLASH. The solution to the problem! If I could make everyone in our class like each other, Mrs Bright might decide that I'm really not a little mischief maker.

So, I'm going to have a party! At my place. And EVERYBODY will be invited. I'm working on Mum to get permission.

Tuesday

Mrs Bright has rearranged our seats. We have to sit where we're told and every week we'll be moved. The idea is that we will learn to get on with everybody else and not just stay with our clubs. I think my idea is better, but you can't tell teachers anything.

I'm next to Rodney. He measured the desk and ruled a line down the middle. He calls it the Demarcation Line. Every time my stuff goes over the line he shoves it back. And if my elbow goes over, he whacks it with his ruler. He shoved my marker pens so hard they flew all over the floor during the spelling test. Mrs Bright looked at me with tight lips. I feel virtuous (my newest word) because I never said a thing about it being Rodney's fault. Rodney will NOT ruin my plans.

But Mum might. She has about seventy-five reasons why I can't have a party. So I'm meeting the boys at lunchtime and we're planning seventy-five arguments to her seventy-five objections.

Wednesday

Poor Sam. He got put next to Skye. He told her that if she tried to help him he would put a frog down her tunic. Then he copied Rodney's idea and drew a demarcation line. He can't measure properly so Skye has about twice as much room as he does but he says he doesn't care as long as she stays on her own side.

I told Mum that I will never, ever, even for my eighteenth birthday, ever ask for another party. AND I will clean up my room in advance. AND I won't ask for any more pocket money this year. AND I will do all the preparations.

She's going to think about it. That's better than no, seventy-five times.

Thursday

Vincent has to sit with Megan. She's sulking because she wants to sit next to Rodney. She keeps turning round in her seat and staring at me to see if I'm trying to steal him. I'd tell her there is no danger, if she'd listen. Vincent thinks it's a great joke. He pretends he's in love with Megan and stares at her. She sits leaning away from him so he leans toward her. He's trying to make her lean so far she'll fall off her seat.

I told Mum that the party is a project for school. Well, it's sort of true. It's a project to improve social relations in Class 5B. And to improve teacher/student relations between Jillian J. and Mrs B.

Friday

Raymond's on detention. Kirrily complained that he was deliberately making smells. Mrs Bright asked him what he was up to and he said it wasn't his fault, he made his own dinner last night when his mum was out. He had a tin of baked beans, a plate of fried onions and some garlic bread. He tried to look all innocent but he's a hopeless actor. Mrs Bright sent him to the loo but that didn't do much good. Every time Kirrily does something that Ray decides is a put-down, he pays her back. We had to open the windows.

Mum says maybe a party would be a good idea. She would like to meet my little girl friends as well as my little boy mates.

Jillian
I must say a party seems a positive step to establishing friendships. Well done. But please do not encourage Raymond and Vincent to be antisocial.
Mrs Bright

Monday

When I grow up I might be a politician. I must have what it takes to be Prime Minister because I've talked Mum into letting me have the party. If I can do that, running the country would be a breeze.

The party's on the weekend after next. The

conditions are that I have to do the preparations and the cleaning up. And I have to put up with Richard and Paul. Locking them in their rooms for the party is not an option.

Nigel and Ray and Sam are going to help. Raymond wants to be the Bouncer and beat up anyone who puts me down. Nigel wants to be Master of Ceremonies. I think that's like a circus ringmaster. Sam wants to be a clown and entertain the crowd. I hope I can convince them my party is not a circus.

I spent all weekend making the invitations. There's one for every person in the class. Even Skye. When she had her party she invited every girl except me and she gave the invitations out in front of me. THAT'S what I call a put-down. Mum said something about how I should turn the other cheek. I think that means let her do the same thing again. I certainly am not going to do the same thing BACK to her, though. I hope she feels ashamed.

The invitations look like this:

WHO'S INVITED You

WHERE Jillian James's place

WHEN Saturday 2pm to whenever!

WHY So 5B can all learn to get along.

BRING Warm clothes
Good Moods
BIG smiles

DON'T BRING Frowns
Put-Downs

I'm giving them out at lunchtime.

Tuesday

First I went to Cat Territory where Kirrily and Company were rehearsing. They looked at the invitations as if they had something slimy squashed on them. Then they looked at each other and started whispering in a huddle. I could only hear a few words: " . . . are you?" and "I don't want. . . "

I started getting hot and angry. Then I started getting that awful swelling lump in my throat. I turned to walk away and Ashley said, "Jillian, what will we be doing there?" Ashley's nicer than the others and sounded pretty friendly. She was doing the dance steps while she spoke and that gave me an idea.

I said, "Well, Ashley, it IS a class party, so we should all contribute. Why don't you get Kirrily and Company to put on your song and dance?"

She said they would let me know the next day.

The boys took their invitations when I said there would be food. They're all coming. Amanda will go if the boys do and the normal kids will go if their parents let them. I told them that my parents and my big brother in high school will all be on hand to supervise. I didn't tell them that Richard can't be trusted to be civilized or that Mum and Dad are planning to order pizza and shut themselves in their room with the TV while the party's on.

Wednesday

They're ALL coming. Even the Princesses. They're coming on condition they can perform. EVERYONE wants to perform. So I said OK, after we've played and had music and eaten the goodies we can have a concert. Nigel says the Master of Ceremonies has to announce the acts.

Mrs Bright moved us again today. She couldn't stand the complaints before, but it's no better now. I'm next to Skye, Sam's next to Rodney, Sarah's got Raymond and Kirrily's got Vincent. Megan and Amanda are together. They hate each other almost as much as Skye hates me. They both sit as far away from each other as they can.

Everyone in the class has ruled demarcation lines down the desks now and we all hold our rulers ready to whack elbows when Mrs Bright isn't looking. Nigel went and bought a ruler with a metal strip along the edge. He calls it his Deadly Weapon of Revenge. Karlie hardly dares to move.

Mrs Bright says that since we're all so interested in rulers all of a sudden, we can practise measuring in millimetres and converting them to centimetres and writing them as fractions of a metre. We got a whole list of things we have to measure.

My Secrets Book is 310 millimetres long which is 31 centimetres which is 0.31 metres. I think.

Thursday

We went to the town library to discuss plans. Nigel insists on calling it a Party Organization Committee Meeting. Raymond told him to shut it. He did.

The librarian saw us come in and started standing near us wherever we went. She kept looking at Raymond and Vincent, and her eyes went bulgy and she looked nervous. I can't really blame her for being scared of them but what did she think they were going to do? Steal her books?!

Sam's eyes nearly popped out of his head. He's never noticed the books before. He usually just heads for the toys or the computers. But now, since he's read a book, he's conscious of them so Nigel and I took him to the librarian's desk and joined him up. His borrower's card will be ready next week. We helped him find a book and I borrowed it for him on my card. The book Sam chose is about dinosaurs. It has a lot of pictures of T-rexes ripping diplodocuses to bits. I grew out of dinosaurs when I was in Year Two but Sam's a slower developer so I didn't say anything. We're going to read it together this weekend.

The librarian got sick of us pretty quickly and said we could talk in the conference room. It has a really thick door, so the library people can't hear us. It was great.

We decided that everyone could dump their jackets and stuff in my bedroom. We'll set up a table out the back and pile it with food so kids won't keep going in and out, and the parents might stay out of the way. With any luck Richard and Paul will stay inside if we give them a plate of goodies.

We'll have chips and cheezies and marshmallows and lollies and fizzy drink. We'll get paper plates and cups to save washing up. And we're making decorations this week. The concert will be under the tree house tree.

Friday

Vincent had a great idea. Near his street there's a sweet factory and it has a shop that sells the lollies they can't put into normal shops. They are called seconds. Vincent calls them deformed lollies. They're really cheap. We're going there after school to buy supplies for the party. We'll have heaps and heaps. And we're going to buy balloons and crepe paper on the way home.

I'm making a list of Things To Do while I'm on detention today after I finish the measurement homework I forgot to do last night. Ray and Sam and Vincent are on detention too. Nigel isn't, he didn't forget. There are still some

flat and squashed. We call them road kill. There are chocolates with the filling oozing out. And message lollies with the messages only half stamped on them. We've got lollies that went the wrong colour, like frogs that are brown because the green and the red colourings were both poured in. We call them toads.

We bought heaps of bags of crisps and we've decided to put them all in a bucket and mix them together so the girls can't just hog the light and tangy flavour. Barbeque, plain, salt and vinegar and light and tangy all in together. Something for everyone. We might do the same with the fizzy drinks. Cola, red soda, orange and lemonade all mixed up. If we can find a big enough container.

Richard volunteered to do the balloons for us. I said OK, that's a good job for someone who's full of hot air. He must be getting nicer, though, offering to help like that.

Wednesday

Vincent got sent home today. He really went too far, even to revenge himself on Kirrily. She called him Gorilla Face. He complained to Mrs Bright that Kirrily made a put-down and Mrs Bright believed Kirrily when she said she didn't, she said Gorgeous Face. Mrs Bright said that Vincent shouldn't always think the worst of people.

Vincent was MAD. He got his pencil and sharpened it with his penknife so the lead was long and sharp like a needle. When Kirrily laid her arm on the table over the demarcation line he put the pencil on the desk pointing towards Kirrily's arm and he put his elbow on it. Then he shoved his arm over and the pencil jammed into Kirrily's wrist and the lead snapped off. You should have heard her squeal! There was a bit of blood. Mrs Bright was so angry!

Vincent got all upset and yelled that it was an accident and Mrs Bright shouldn't think the worst of him all the time. So she KNEW he'd done it deliberately and dragged him off to Mr Bigg. Kirrily's mother had to come and get her because she was hysterical.

The room is really quiet now. Nobody dares whisper or move. Mrs Bright's face is all white except for two spots of red on her cheeks. Her eyes remind me of the raptors' in Sam's book.

Thursday

Kirrily is back at school today. She's got her arm bandaged from her thumb up to her shoulder and she's got it in a sling. She's limping too. That's too much to swallow, even for Mrs Bright. She asked Kirrily how a minor wound in the lower arm could cause a limp and necessitate a sling. Kirrily burst into tears. That's her strategy when she can't think of an answer. Mrs Bright got impatient and went off to try again to teach Sam about the "igh" word family.

Kirrily started smirking as soon as Mrs Bright left. I leant over and whispered, "Gee,

Kirrily, I hope your injuries don't prevent you performing with the Company on Saturday!" Kirrily's got a worried look on her face now. Ha.

Vincent didn't come back to school today.

Friday

Kirrily walked in normally this morning. Her arm was out of the sling and the bandage only went from the wrist to the elbow. She made faces every time she moved and groaned to show she was in pain but was being very brave about it. Mrs Bright told her to stop the groaning and if she had a stomach ache to go to the toilet. Everyone giggled and now Kirrily's sulking. She says she's not coming to the you-know-what tomorrow. She's too ill. The other Princesses are having a breakdown about how they'll do the dance without Kirrily. Skye looks sort of pleased though.

Vincent came back to school today but he has to sit by himself at a desk next to Mrs

Bright's. He's on time-out for the rest of term. He won't speak to anyone. Even me. I hope he comes to the party. I gave him one of the message lollies. But I'm not telling what it had written on it.

Dear Jillian
    I hope your party is a success. I'm so pleased with your measurement work. You're really getting the hang of the decimal system.
    Mrs Bright

Monday

A REPORT ON JILLIAN JAMES'S PARTY
By Jillian James. 5B.

This is an assignment set by Mrs Bright. If I had my way I would never think about that party again. And I certainly would never write about it.

A report is supposed to be a factual

description of events in the order they happened, with a comment about the good and the bad points.

Well, Mrs Bright, you might as well give me a C without reading this report. I'm too churned up to think about events in order. My comments would be unprintable. And there are no good points in total, utter disaster.

THE BEGINNING OF THE END OF MY SOCIAL LIFE

Hours and hours of preparation. We cleared up my room. We shoved all the junk under the bed and pulled the covers down so they touched the floor. We threw all the clothes and shoes and books and my shell collection and my pine cone collection into the wardrobe and slammed the door shut before it all fell out again. We tried to vacuum the floor and got up most of the glitter shapes, except for where the glue spilt on the carpet during last holidays.

Then we got the backyard ready. Vincent

and Raymond took the picnic table out and set it up. Sam pooper-scooped where Fang had been. I started hanging the kilometre of paper chains from tree to tree and around the fence. I yelled to Richard to bring out the balloons and he yelled back, "All in good time, my petal." I should have heard alarm bells then.

It was about lunchtime by then so we started getting the food ready. We had two plastic buckets full of mixed chips. The only container big enough for the drink was Paul's old baby bath but he doesn't need it any more so that was OK. We washed it out and put it ready on the table.

We mixed the lollies on the plates. Siamese twins and roadkill and message lollies and oozing chocolates and marshmallows all together. We didn't eat too many because we didn't want to be sick for the party.

Mum made heaps of sausage rolls and cream-filled fairy cakes, which was a lovely surprise. I think she was so pleased that I was trying so hard that she decided I deserved some reward.

Then we hung sheets down from the tree house to be a background for the concert. And finally we all went to change into our party clothes.

Tuesday

THE DESPERATE MIDDLE

While I was having a shower I heard Richard go out into the backyard to put up the balloons. I combed my hair and put on my good embroidered jeans, my clean joggers and my new red sweatshirt. The boys had come back by then so we all went outside to wait.

Up until then everything had been going well.

There is an old saying that "Pride goes before a fall." It's true, because I was just starting to feel great when the slings and arrows of outrageous fortune started flying in all directions. I couldn't lie down to sleep or to dream. I was in a nightmare already. And I couldn't boldly fight against them either. There were too many all at once. I had to nobly suffer them.

About ten kids arrived all at once, just as I noticed Paul. He had climbed onto the table and was dropping flat jelly babies into the fizzy drink. He was saying, "Swim, bubba, swim." I ran to grab him and turned around to say hello to the kids. They were looking at the balloons. Richard had hung them everywhere—but up high where I couldn't reach. Each balloon had a drawing and writing in marker pen. Everyone was reading and giggling. So I went to see what Richard had written.

I can't write down what he wrote because this report is being written in a No Put-Down Zone. Richard has obviously been snooping in my Secrets Book and has remembered my alliteration sentences. No-one in my class escaped.

Wednesday

IT GETS WORSE

Kirrily and Company arrived last of all. They all came together. And they all wore the same clothes: their little shiny tops and miniskirts. And they all had exactly the same number of waggly clips in their hair. A dozen each. They had body glitter love-hearts on their cheeks and each had two letters painted on their foreheads.

Kirrily had ^K_C , Megan had ^Y_Y ,

Skye had ^R_P , Karlie had ^L_N ,

Sara had ^I_O , Juliet had ^I_A

and Ashley had ^R_M

    Everyone kept asking if they were boys' initials or a secret code or what, but they wouldn't tell.

Nigel started bossing and told everyone to come and mingle and start eating. They did. I took Paul inside to change him out of his wet clothes. It took longer than it should have because excitement always means a big nappy job for Paul.

When I got outside again, Skye, Kirrily and Juliet were crying in a corner, with all the other girls, except Amanda, cuddling them. Raymond had made sure they read their balloons. In fact he had got them down and personally delivered them.

Then Rodney started screaming that the drink was in a baby bath and was a funny colour and it must have germs. So Sam kicked him in the knee. Rodney went to the corner to cry with Kirrily and Co. Vincent started calling out that they were wusses. Skye screamed that he was Nigellated. So Nigel got upset and started to walk home.

By the time I convinced him to come back inside the fence, all the girls and Rodney were on one side of the yard and all the boys and Amanda were in the tree house, which was creaking and ready to collapse. Richard was sitting on the patio roof reciting alliteration poems and Paul was playing swimming in the baby bath again. Only this time it was Paul swimming, not flat jelly babies.

Thursday

AND WORSE

I couldn't nobly suffer any more. It was too much to bear. So I did the only thing possible. I ran inside and slammed the door on the whole disaster. Just as I was getting to my room Dad appeared, on his way to the kitchen. He asked how it was going and then he saw my face. He didn't say another word. He just grabbed my arm and dragged me out the back with him.

After one look around he took control. He reached up and grabbed Richard by the foot and hauled him down. Then he fished Paul out of the drink. He shut Paul and Richard inside the house.

He tipped out the drink (what was left of it.) He roared at the boys to get down. NOW! They did. He called the girls over. They came. He just stood there with his hands on his hips and stared around at everyone. Everyone stared back, like you do at a dog that's about to attack you. Rodney sniffled, and that broke the silence. Dad never yells. Well, hardly ever. Mum yells but when Dad is really mad he talks soft. It's dead scary, much scarier than Mum yelling.

He said, "Well, kids, it takes every guest to make a party. Jillian here has gone to a lot of trouble to prepare it for you and now it's your turn to help make today a good time. So let's get started, eh?"

They all said, "Yes, Mr James." Together, like they were in school.

I love my dad.

Friday

MORE

Dad made us play Simon Says and Musical Chairs till we were all smiling. Then he made up a game where you had to sit on balloons until they burst. That destroyed the poetry and made us all laugh. Then Dad told us time was marching on so we'd better have our concert. And he went inside and Nigel took over.

Nigel organized us to sit around the patio where we could Partake Of Party Food And Enjoy The Spectacle.

Sam was on first. He did magic tricks that nobody could understand but we all clapped madly. We didn't want him running off or my dad coming out again.

Rodney recited a poem he had learned for an Eisteddfod. It was all about flowers and rainbows and he said it in a posh voice. The girls thought it was sooooo cute. I had to stare really hard at Vincent and hold on to Raymond's arm because I had a feeling they wanted to say something very rude.

Then Ray and Vincent said it was their turn. Nigel said it wasn't, it was Amanda's turn to do cartwheels and flips. But they pushed Nigel into his seat and stood and took turns to tell limericks. Each limerick was ruder than the one before. I was scared Dad would come out and hear. But I was sort of hoping he would come out, too. We were embarrassed but some of the limericks were pretty funny and we started giggling. I've put the best ones into my Secrets Book.

After Amanda's gymnastics and Nigel's song and Brendan's riddles, it was time for Kirrily and Company. Nigel announced it as the Grand Finally.

The girls stood in a row. They were shivering because it was getting late and the sun was going down. They kept looking sideways at each other and giggling. Then they counted one, two, three and started. They were supposed to move to the left to start but Megan went right and knocked Skye over. Karlie fell on top of them. The boys began to whistle and clap and Kirrily screamed at them. I helped them up and they started again.

They sang this song with words that don't make sense but it's really big on the radio. They did these steps where they have to go left and right and then forwards and backwards and then in and out around each other. Then at the end they ended up in a line and pointed to their foreheads.

I finally got it. If they had got into the proper order, their foreheads would have spelled out:

K I R R I L Y

C O M P A N Y

But they got it wrong. They spelled

L I K I R R Y

N O C A M P Y

I couldn't help it. I read it out loud.

Ray started laughing. So did Nigel and Sam. Then Amanda. Then even Rodney. Then everyone else, except the Company. Vincent pelted Kirrily with a road kill and it hit her on the bare leg. She squealed and picked it up and threw it back. It hit Raymond so he grabbed a handful of Siamese twins and pelted everyone in the Company.

As the old saying goes, all hell broke loose. Slings and arrows, lollies and cream cakes flew everywhere. Screams and yells filled the air.

THE BITTER END

I spent all day Sunday cleaning up. Richard had to help. I am never allowed to have a party again. I don't care. I don't WANT to. The boys aren't allowed to come over in the foreseeable future. I don't care. I can't talk to anyone.

Jillian,
    Things may not be as bad as you think. Stop hiding away!
    Mrs Bright

Monday

Last Monday, when I started my report, I wrote that there were no good points in total, utter disaster. I was wrong.

When we read out our reports this morning, Sam, Vincent, Raymond, Amanda and Brendan all said that it was the best party they've ever been to. Jamie wrote that mixed chips taste fabulous. Half the kids have started bringing Siamese twins and road kill for recess. Rodney said it's the first time he's felt accepted as one of the crowd at any of the schools he's been to.

Rodney came and asked if he could play soccer with Sam and me this morning. After I got Raymond to swear he wouldn't kick him we let him join in. Nigel sulked for a while, then he cheered up when he realized that Rodney misses kicks even more than he does.

Kirrily and Company were really shirty about Rodney, but Kirrily said that she never realized before what I have to put up with at home, not having brothers herself. The other

Princesses agreed. Skye wants me to take a letter from her to Richard. I said I would if she promised to be kinder to me and my friends. She agreed, so she must be in love with Richard. Skye and Megan have got "RJ is a spunk" written on their pencil cases. Gross.

Mum came to school last week and had a long interview with Mrs Bright. I don't know what they said but they both had tight lips for days. Then Mrs Bright changed the seats and put me next to Rodney again.

We are all working in pairs now. Our seat partner is our Work Buddy. She seems to have matched us with kids who get the same sort of marks. Vincent is with Sam. Raymond is with Amanda. Nigel is by himself. Rodney is great at reading and writing. He's pretty good at maths, too. Like me.

Tuesday

I keep noticing more good outcomes from the disaster. (*Outcome* is a teacher word for *result*.)

I'm writing limericks now. But I'm being very careful.

There was an old lady named Bright,
Who got up in the dead of the night.
Looked in the mirror to see,
Thought to herself "Is that me?"
And got one hell of a fright.

(No offence, Mrs B. It's a joke!)

Amanda has joined our soccer group and wants to come over when I'm allowed to have kids around again.

Dad said he doesn't know how I stand going to school every day with that pack of whining little ninnies (that's the princesses). Mum said she understands now why I seem to prefer the boys' company. And she knows now why I keep saying Richard is a pain. Richard is grounded until he writes an apology to every kid in my class. And he has to take over Paul-changing duty. He says he's going to introduce Paul to the potty on the weekend.

Wednesday

I've only just realized that the holidays are around the corner. I'm going to be really good so Mum will let me have friends around again.

Skye keeps smiling at me and wanting to be my friend so she can come round and flutter her eyelashes at Richard. This gives me a dilemma. Earlier in the year I would have done ANYTHING to be a Princess and hang around with Skye. Now the idea is boring. But I don't want to upset Mrs Bright by saying so, or risk starting another war. On the other hand I don't want to lose my other friends. And why should I help Richard with his love life after all he's done? I'd better make lists of the pros and cons and come to a decision.

Thursday

This morning I gave Skye the sealed envelope with Richard's reply. (Wish I had X-ray vision.) I told Skye that I am perfectly prepared to be friendly with her but it would be on my terms. She asked what I meant and I said, "Take me, and take my friends. Take me as I am, because I'm not going to change for you or any other Princess."

She looked surprised and said she'd have to think about it. Then she ran off to the other girls. They've been whispering and looking at me. It's strange, I couldn't care less if she says yes or no.

Rodney and Nigel are teaching me and Amanda how to publish on the computer. We're thinking of writing a newsletter.

Friday

On the weekend we're going to the library to plan. Nigel says the librarian will let us use her conference room again. There will be Sam, me, Vincent, Ray, Amanda and Rodney as well as Nige. We might even do a magazine during the holidays. We're busting with ideas. And we're changing Sam's library books too.

Jillian,

The newsletter idea sounds marvellous. The boys have been blossoming lately with their literacy skills. If you need any advice, just ask.

Mrs Old Lady named Bright

Monday

Skye, Megan, Kirrily and Juliet have started a new club called the ARL. They asked me if I'd like to join and I almost did because I thought it was a football club. But Skye was smiling her "in love" smile and I got suspicious. They don't follow football. So I asked what the club was about. I decided not to join when I found out that ARL means the Association Of Richard Lovers. As if! But I agreed to carry their notes in return for friendly behaviour.

Sam used his borrower's card on Saturday. He borrowed six books. I showed him where the easier chapter books for beginner readers are and we found some that aren't too babyish. He's read one already. Raymond and Vincent started looking at the books too. I showed them the shelves of sports books. I had to borrow one on Rugby League for Ray and one on martial arts for Vincent. Then we helped them fill out borrower's join-up cards.

We didn't get to have our meeting though. The librarian threw us out when Vincent found a book about the human body in the biology section and the boys started giggling at the pictures. Amanda and I went to the park. We decided that boys really are pathetic.

Tuesday

Mrs Bright seems happy today. She wrote on the board, "Only four to go!" Just like one of the kids. Rodney asked her what teachers do in holiday breaks. She smiled and said, "Teachers plot and plan during holidays. While you children are busily forgetting all you've learned, we teachers are remembering all you don't know and planning lessons for you to come back to. Oh, I've so many ideas I don't know where to begin!"

We all groaned. I put up my hand and said that she deserved a holiday as much as we do and she should take a good long rest. Rodney called ME a sycophant!

I'm not. I really meant it.

Wednesday

The chalkboard says, "3 days to go!" Mrs Bright's smile is getting brighter. She's doing a lot of writing at her desk. We're doing a lot of worksheets with word puzzles and mixed mentals on them. I love them. They're so easy, I get plenty of ·reading time. Richard lent me his Sherlock Holmes books a couple of weeks ago. I'm addicted to them. I might be a detective when I grow up. Or at least a detective story writer. Rodney's reading Sherlock Holmes too.

Thursday

Mum has lifted the ban on friends for the holidays as long as everything is satisfactory.

I've been cleaning up my room—properly this time. I got a big plastic bag that you put gardening rubbish into and some cardboard boxes from the back of the shops. I'm working my way around the room. Dirty clothes go into the basket. Rubbish into the bag. Pine cones into one box. Shells into another. Dead lunches into the bag. Books into a huge pile on the bed to sort out later. I have to sleep around the pile. (It's a bit uncomfortable, but Dad's right when he says he has chronically lazy offspring.) Shoes into a fruit box. All the pencils and pens and rubbers into a decorated box I got for Christmas once. My ornament collection into yet another box. Except the broken ones I've been going to fix for years. They're going into the garbage bag. All the glitter and glue and stickers and paper and stuff into a useful box.

Mum says my intentions are good, but to

remember that the Road To Hell Is Paved With Good Intentions. I think she's warning me I might not get my friends over if I don't finish the job.

Friday

The board says, "LAST DAY! HOORAY!" We all agree, most heartily!

We've cleaned out our desks and handed in our books. We played games and had Assembly.

I have finally worked out why Mrs Bright has been so busy and so happy.

And what Mum has been waiting for.

It's sitting on my desk now. In a sealed envelope, addressed to Mum and Dad.

The Teacher's Revenge.

My School Report.

Term Three

Monday

A PROCEDURE, by Jillian James

<u>HOW TO HAVE A GREAT HOLIDAY</u>

(I don't want to do another report on my holidays, Mrs Bright, or a narrative, so I'm trying a procedure.)

WHAT YOU NEED:

* A good school report.
* A happy mum.
* Preferably no brothers.
* Friends who can be civilised in a public library.

STEPS TO FOLLOW:

1. To get the bans lifted:
   a. Take home report and tell Mum how hard you've been working. Get out fast.
   b. Make sure parents see your tidy room, and make them breakfast on first day.
   c. Be pleasant to big brother when he teases you about friends who happen to be boys. Make little brother's breakfast without being asked.

d. Sit and write list of educational activities for holiday fun with friends. Leave where parents can see and be impressed.

e. Keep fingers crossed.

2. Once bans on friends are lifted:

a. Meet friends out back and make them promise to speak politely, not yell, tease anyone or eat all the food.

b. Arrange to meet at everyone's house in turn so parents don't go mad.

c. Check parents carefully each morning for mood before asking for anything. Do at least one job before going out.

3. When you get freedom:

a. Be VERY polite to librarian. Learn to speak quietly.

b. Let Nigel think he's in charge and let him tell everyone what to do. Then go ahead and do what you really want to.

c. Put Vincent in charge of sports news;
Raymond in charge of video news;
Sam in charge of artwork;
Amanda in charge of puzzles;
Jillian in charge of book reviews and news.

And make Rodney the publication manager.

d. Think of a good magazine title. DON'T argue about names at top of voices when Mum is watching movie.

e. Have plenty of paper for drafts.

f. Buy lots of deformed lollies from factory shop.

4. When first issue of "Slings and Arrows" is ready to print:

a. Be sure you saved your files.

b. Use a mysterious password so big brothers can't get into the files and change important words which you don't discover until the copies have been run off.

c. Be sure your dad knows you're using all his colour printer ink.

d. Have enough paper to run off new copies without big brother's alterations.

e. Do NOT let Raymond sit and toss your pet rock up and down near computer monitor.

5. When your magazine is finally printed:

a. Keep copies for mum, teacher and librarian. And one for yourself.
b. Try to sell the rest to classmates.
c. Muck about for the rest of break.
d. Do lots of car-washing, babysitting, lawn-mowing etc to earn money to pay for new printer ink, paper and computer monitor.

Tuesday

The librarian has our magazine on display in the Library. She says she's very proud of our effort. We're going to give her another copy though, because someone's blacked out parts of Vincent's sports stories. We gave Mrs Bright her copy yesterday. She was reading it when she was on playground duty. She got a coughing fit while she was reading it. Her shoulders were shaking and she was making a choking noise.

She liked our magazine. She said it was a unique document.

Our sales have risen to ten. Each of us got our parents to buy their copy. That's seven. The other three were bought by Kirrily, Brendan and a kid in Year Four who wants to be in Kirrily's group.

The Princesses say our magazine is boring. They all read Kirrily's copy. They say we should write stories about kids who have interesting hobbies. Like singing and dancing. After all our work I felt pretty cranky, so I suggested that Kirrily might like to write her own article and publish it for all her fans. Raymond made a suggestion too, but I can't repeat it. Kirrily repeated it when she went crying to Mrs Bright. Raymond is on detention and it's only the first week back.

Wednesday

Yesterday at assembly Mr Bigg announced that this term is Athletics Carnival Term. We usually have it in Second Term but this year they're trying to get a time when it's not raining or freezing or so windy we get blown away.

Athletics Carnival is something I have tried to blot out of my mind all year. Last year I took my book and hid behind a tree for most of the day, reading, until Melissa told on me and I was forced to go in my age race. (Even though I told the teacher I was a conscientious objector to competition and did not believe in pitting my physical talents against others.)

We have to have HOUSE MEETINGS this afternoon.

Thursday

At Flora Heights Primary we have four sports houses. They are: WARATAH (red); WATTLE (yellow); PLUMBAGO (blue); ORCHID (green).

I'm in Wattle House. So are Nigel and Sam. We had to go to Mr Connors' room for our meeting. The captains are Stuart and Amelia. Stuart is like Vincent (violent) and Amelia is a Year Six Kirrily clone. Our House teacher is Miss Evans. She's only been teaching for about a year so she's still enthusiastic about carnivals and excursions.

She went on for ages about House Spirit and Striving For Excellence. It all boiled down to one thing. She's forcing every person in Wattle to enter or at least try out for EVERY event. We get a point for participating and extra points for getting a place. The only place I ever get is last but you don't get points for that.

Then she said we all have to make up a War Cry and we'll vote for the best one on Friday. It has to show the True Wattle Spirit.

I can't run. But, Mrs Bright, I'll be positive. I'll do a War Cry because I CAN write.

Friday

My War Cry goes like this:

> *Green are our leaves, gold are our flowers.*
> *We have trained for hours and hours*
> *To do our best and win the battle.*
> *Come on, team, the mighty Wattle!*

Amelia and Stuart say it stinks. Amelia says that battle and wattle don't rhyme and anyway you can't do a good dance to it. Stuart wants a War Cry that has words about crushing other teams. Miss Evans made us all vote for her favourite, which she had at her primary school. It goes:

Extra, extra, read all about it!
We've got a team and there's no
doubt about it.
Gotta shout it from the east and
shout it from the west—
Come on Wattle, you're the best!

I have an awful sinking feeling in my tummy, that this year's Athletics Carnival is going to be a disaster.

Jillian,
    Please don't let sour grapes spoil your enjoyment of the Carnival. Remember, POSITIVE TRACKING!
    Mrs Bright

Monday

Positive Tracking is Mrs Bright's new Big Idea. It follows on from No Put-Downs. It means you have to look on the bright side of disasters and find a good thing in them. So here goes.

* Miss Evans' War Cry will be good for Amelia's cheer squad to dance to. She's got the little kids spying on Waratah because Kirrily is making up their dance.
* No-one can blame me if we don't win the War Cry. I didn't write it.
* The Athletics Carnival will be over in three weeks. If it doesn't get postponed due to rain or snow or something.

Amelia is holding auditions for the War Cry dance today at lunch. I told her that dancing is against my beliefs but Miss Evans said I talk rubbish and should show better Team Spirit.

Tuesday

Positive thought for the day:

- ★ Amelia refuses to have sour-faced people with two left feet in HER cheer squad. That puts me and Nigel out. So we can do something more interesting at lunchtimes for the next three weeks. Like watch the grass grow.

Yesterday we started Marching Practice. Miss Evans, Amelia and Stuart made us line up in rows of three, from shortest to tallest. I'm in a row with the Teddy twins who are the shortest kids in Year Four. We call them the Teddies because they're short and cute and—well—cuddly. And they have curly brown hair.

I have to march in between them because they smile and I sulk. Then everyone sees them on the outside and not me skulking and sulking along in the middle. Stuart saw me though. He thumped me because I was going right, left, right, left, right, left when everyone else was going left, right, left, right, left, right. He said I wasn't working as a team.

Wednesday

Nigel has to march in the second back row with Year Six kids. The boy behind him keeps treading on his heel. He had to stop yesterday to put his shoe back on and Stuart thumped him and Amelia screamed at him for ruining the team.

Positive thought: At least Adam the Crusher who weighs two tonnes is in Orchid House!

After Marching we had to try out for Ball Game teams. Miss Evans made us all be in one of the two teams. The little kids do over and under ball and the big kids do bob ball and tunnel ball.

I missed out on bob ball. When Stuart chucked the ball at me I was just about to pick the scab on my elbow so the ball hit me in the face. After my nose stopped bleeding Miss Evans said I'd be better suited to a game where the ball rolls along the ground.

Lauren Ball is in charge of tunnel ball. I like that, her name suits the job. We spent 30 minutes and 47 seconds (according to Nigel's stopwatch) practising standing up straight and making a tunnel EXACTLY 40cm wide, every foot in a straight line, moving RIGHT foot only, then standing straight up again. Over and over and over.

We might get to roll a ball today.

Thursday

The boys came round after school yesterday. Amanda is in Orchid house. She's in their tunnel ball AND their bob ball teams. I was sorry for her but she says only the BEST players get chosen in her house so it's an honour to make the teams. She's sorry for me only being in one team!

Raymond is in Plumbago. He got into trouble for calling it Bumbago at their first House meeting so he says he's not going to cooperate now. He got put out of marching for tripping up the girls. He spent their Ball Game try-outs in the tree pelting Plumbago with gumnuts. He hates Athletics Carnivals too.

So does Sam. He got forced into the tunnel ball team with Nigel and me. He hates being pressed against other kids because they tell him he's got potatoes growing in his ears. Nigel and I both have a habit of moving our left foot instead of our right so we have to practise more in tunnel making until we can learn to work as a team.

Vincent is in Waratah. He says it's been fun so far. He suggested a War Cry but got put on detention because it was so rude. And when Kirrily started making up their dance he told kids in Year Six about the dance at my party. Now he goes along to all their practices and copies their moves. He's going to sell their dance to the highest bidder.

Positive thought: At least Amanda and Vincent are happy about the Carnival.

Friday

Some people get all the luck. Yesterday Mrs Bright took our class out for shotput practice before the try-outs. The shotput is a really, REALLY heavy metal ball. You have to throw it as far as you can. That's called putting the shot. The school record holder is Adam the Crusher, who can put an awful lot of weight behind his throws.

My effort wasn't too bad. I got it about 1.8 metres, which was only about a metre behind the second last girl. Nigel's first throw went about 90 cm. Mrs Bright got really mad at the kids who laughed at him. She said he must have dropped it and said he could have a second go. Ray picked it up and threw it over to Nigel. Nigel is in the tunnel ball team because he still can't catch a basket ball. He didn't stand a chance. The shot landed on his foot. (The left one that's always sticking out into the wrong place.)

Nigel's foot will be in plaster for weeks. He won't be able to be in tunnel ball or any other event at the Carnival. Raymond will be allowed to return to school next Monday. He said he was only trying to help Nigel, but Mrs Bright said he hasn't got a chance of attending the Carnival unless he can find some Team Spirit.

Maybe I can fall out of the tree house on the weekend and break a leg.

Jillian,
    Where is your Positive Tracking? You seem to be forgetting YOUR team spirit, too.
    Mrs Bright

Monday

Rodney made a big sign for our classroom on the weekend. It has the words:

ALWAYS LOOK ON THE *BRIGHT* SIDE.

He drew pictures of smiling children looking at a teacher. The drawings even look like some people in our class. Mrs Bright LOVES it. (You slimy sycophant, Rodney.)

She says she appreciates the pun. A pun is when you use a word so it has two meanings at the same time. Like the thankyou card Rodney made me after the party. There was a cat saying "Thankyou for the purrrfectly lovely time."

Now Nigel and Rodney and I keep putting puns into our conversation. Mrs Bright even smiled when she overheard one of them. I had said that being electrocuted must be a *shocking* experience. Punny—I mean, Funny, eh?

Later I told her that my brother Richard wants to change his last name to Tator. She asked why and I said because kids call him Dick. She told me to get on with my work and her lips went all thin.

I don't think she got the pun.

Tuesday

Plumbago have had trouble coming up with a War Cry. They couldn't get rhymes for plumbago, except for sago and lumbago, which aren't good war cry words.

But Raymond–RAYMOND!!!! Of all people!!! has made up a War Cry for them and sent Vincent to give it to them. I don't know the words because it's top secret. They crowd into Mrs Bright's room and shut the windows and doors and pull down the blinds. A lot of yelling comes through the walls but the words aren't clear. They say it's clean, even if Raymond did write it. It can't be that good, though. Raymond isn't up to sentences with commas yet.

I'm confused. If Raymond isn't co-operating, why is he writing a War Cry? Is he going soft? I asked him yesterday after school but he just smirked and said to wait and see. Sometimes he reminds me of Richard.

Our War Cry dance squad are going to dress up as gumnut babies in green clothes and yellow crepe paper hats and skirts.

When I said that wattle trees don't produce gumnuts they kicked me out of the practice area. I went to the bottom playground to my old lurking hole to read. But Rodney was already there. He's hiding from the Waratah cheer squad. They want to dress him up as a giant red flower and make him wave handfuls of petals.

Wednesday

Marching practice. Result: two blisters, two sore ears.

Tunnel ball practice. Result: one sore foot from Stuart stamping on out-of-line-feet. And a headache.

War Cry practice. Result: green-ant bites from lurking under bushes.

And now we have to do long jump try-outs! There is a big patch of sand under the trees in the bottom playground. We're supposed to practise at lunchtimes to get our technique right for try-outs. The sporty kids with long legs have been hogging it for two weeks. I haven't bothered bringing my shorts along. It's not like I'd get a go.

Yesterday afternoon, Miss Evans suddenly

should wear it and to go and find something positive to talk about.

I whispered to Sam that I POSITIVELY loathe Athletics Carnivals.

Positive thought. People who get on time-out for smart comments are unable to attend ball game practice at lunch.

(And Mrs Bright, I wasn't being a smartypants. I was making a truthful comment to a friend.)

Friday

Long jump practice. Result: sand in embarrassing parts of my body, sore back, sore head, sore face.

Yesterday afternoon they went on to HIGH JUMPS! I knew I couldn't do it. The only time I've ever done a high jump in my entire life was when we went bushwalking and I nearly stepped on a black snake. I jumped on to Dad's shoulder in terror. I told Miss Evans as politely as I could that it would be a total waste of time trying me out. She wasted even more time giving me a lecture about Team Spirit, and about Participation being more important than Winning. Then she forced me to try out.

First try: I baulked at the first try . . . the one metre jump.

Second try: I sort of jumped but only one leg got over. I landed on top of the bar.

Third try: After they set the bar up again I tried. I REALLY tried. I hobbled up to the bar and I jumped. My knees knocked the bar. I fell. The bar fell. I screamed. You'd scream too, if you came crashing down with your legs tangled around a metal bar.

Miss Evans told me to stop the drama attack and go and sit on a lunch seat.

I am not required to attend high jump practice again. However, since no bones were broken, I AM required to attend the Athletics Carnival.

Dear Jillian

Despite your long face, limping and lurking, I HAVE noticed that you have been participating as a house member. Don't despair about your lack of success. We can't all be Olympians!

A BRIGHT thought from Mrs Bright

Monday

We spent all weekend making signs and shakers for our houses. Rodney's dad has a shredder. We bought plastic bags in blue, yellow and green. We couldn't find red so we had to get orange for Waratah.

You feed the bag through the shredder and it comes out in long thin strips. When you've done lots of bags you have a big pile of strips which you double over, and tape up the folded end to make a handle and you've got a fabulous shaker.

Nigel, Sam and I made yellow ones with a

bit of green for Wattle. Raymond made blue ones for Plumbago. Amanda made the green ones for Orchid and Vincent and Rodney made the Orange Waratah ones.

We made terrific signs, too. Dad's got new colour cartridges now.

We had to destroy Raymond and Vincent's posters. They did not display the Proper Team Spirit.

Tuesday

The Carnival is on this Friday. Only four more days of marching, yelling, running, rolling balls and lurking under bushes. Then it will be back to normal. I could almost welcome a page of long division.

The Cheer Squads all got in trouble yesterday for Engaging in Espionage. I looked it up. It means spying. Someone gave Vincent two dollars to show them Waratah's dance. That was the highest bid. At lunch all these kids were doing Waratah's dance but with extra movements. Vincent showed them how to do the dance while they pointed to their foreheads and bumped into each other.

Kirrily and Skye got it and went crying to Mr Bigg and he kept the whole school in lines for about an hour telling us about Sportsmanship and Team Spirit. Even the teachers started fidgetting. Positive thought: We didn't have time for Marching Practice.

I sat with Vincent on time-out today. It had to be more interesting than watching jumping or ball games.

Wednesday

Nigel is back at school. He's on crutches and his foot is in plaster. He was popular for five minutes while the kids wanted to write their names on his plaster, but that wore off when the plaster got covered.

We spent time-out practising walking with crutches. You never know when you'll need a skill like that.

Raymond's on time-out for the foreseeable future. The teachers are afraid he's planning to take revenge on innocent people.

Thursday

We spent most of today in last-minute preparations for tomorrow. Miss Evans is frantic. Mrs Bright is frazzled. Mr Connors is getting frustrated. I think that rain tomorrow would be great but I'm not that lucky. And anyway, Mr Connors said at Assembly, that "Rain, hail, sleet or snow, Flora Heights' Carnival is sure to go!" Most of the kids cheered. Mrs Bright looked grim. Miss Evans doesn't look as enthusiastic as she used to.

This afternoon we're going to the factory seconds shop to stock up on road kills and Siamese twins to keep up our energy levels tomorrow.

I don't think I'll take my book to read at the carnival. I might take my notebook instead.

Jillian,

I trust that your report on the carnival will be more positive than your lead-up to it. However, the signs and shakers sound very sporting.

Mrs Bright

Monday

My report on Friday's fiasco will be in ballad form.

THE SORRY SAGA OF JILLIAN'S
ATHLETIC ENDEAVOURS

We set out for the oval,
Our march a warlike tramp.
Green, and Red, Blue and Gold
Each set up their base Camp.

The Teachers ranged in front of us,
We heard a hearty bark.
"Get up and get in lines, you lot,
You're marching round the park!"

"Left! Right! Left! Right! Left! Right!"
Our eager Captains cried.
I managed to stay out of sight,
The twins on either side.

We stood anxiously before the judge,
While he made the "Bigg" decision.
Red came first, but we were fourth!
THAT score needs revision!

Next, the hundred metres race:
Kind fortune did not shine.
Bossy Stuart found me
And dragged me to the line.

I lined up with the eleven-year-olds.
I heard my thumping heart.
"This year, THIS year I'll win a race!"
I thought, and missed the start.

Gulping the dust of my rivals,
I plodded down the track.
Before I reached the halfway mark,
They'd started heading back.

Laughter echoed in my ears.
"Go on, Jillian!" they cried.
My legs pumped up, my legs pumped down
But my inner spirit died.

Ball games next. They called to me
To line up with my team.
Stuart pushed me, Amelia pulled me,
Gave orders in a scream.

Seven legs right, one leg left—
"You moron!" Stuart said.
And one leg wrong was all it took;
Victory went to the Red.

Another chance to make some points:
The War Cries! Wattle roared.
We yelled! We shouted! We gave our best!
We smirked, we knew we'd scored.

Next Green, then Red—they were OK;
Then Plumbago stood in a block.
They started in a tiny voice
Which grew; we reeled in shock.

"We're Plumbago, couldn't be prouder,
If you can't hear, we'll sing it out louder!
We're Plumbago, couldn't be prouder,
If you can't hear, we'll sing it out louder!"

Again and
Again and
Again and
Again and Again.

Parents were laughing, teachers were grinning,
"How original!" they all said.
"First place to Blue!" Mr Bigg decided.
And now they tied with Red.

Shotput, jumps and novelties;
We hoped to save our side.
But our score kept way down low;
And with it stayed our pride.

At last we packed up and assembled,
The point scores and places were clear.
First Red, then Blue, with Orchid in third.
Yellow unplaced for another year.

Another Carnival over.
At least for another year.
"Maybe NEXT time," I thought to myself,
"I'll win", and brushed off a tear.

Well, Mrs Bright. That's my report on the Athletics Carnival. I tried a ballad. I'm sorry if you think I'm a bad sport and a mischief maker. I'm not. I'm just paving that road to Hell with my good intentions.

Jillian James

Dear Jillian,

Your ballad was the best part of the whole carnival, in my opinion. But keep that to yourself. As a teacher I am paid to be enthusiastic and encourage the Team Spirit. It is just unfortunate for you that you were not born a team player.

Mrs Bright

Tuesday

We had assembly yesterday afternoon, to see the Athletics Carnival trophies presented and to cheer the winners. Mr Bigg went on and on (again) about how the real meaning of Athletics Carnivals is Team Spirit and Participation.

Well, I was confused. When we got back to class I asked Mrs Bright: if the real meaning is about participating, how come only the winners get trophies and ribbons? She told me to sit down and get on with my work. But I don't think she was angry with me. I think she might have been thinking the same thing, judging by her comment about my poem.

At my place after school we decided to do something positive. We gave each other awards for our participation in the carnival. We didn't give Amanda one. She already has a huge trophy for being Senior Girl Athletics Champion.

Ray got the Poets Award for creating the Most Irritating War Cry of the year. He was rapt.

I got the Black-and-Blue award for

sustaining the most bruises of the carnival. Nigel reckoned his foot was a worse injury until I pointed out that my injuries were emotional as well as physical.

We gave Nigel the Golden Boot for being the cheeriest cheerer. Sam won the Cannibal King award for fitting the largest number of Siamese twins into his mouth at one go. Vincent got the Twinkle Toes award for creative dancing. And Rodney got the Royal Flush award for having a face as red as his Waratah costume in their War Cry Dance.

Rodney's making certificates for us tonight on his computer.

Wednesday

Back to normal. We did long division this morning. I'd forgotten how to do them. Well, actually, I never understood how to do them in the first place. Rodney the maths whizz showed me a magic trick for doing them. You have to follow these steps: Guess, Multiply,

Subtract, Check and Start Again. Keep following the steps and you're OK, if you know your tables.

Mrs Bright said she was pleasantly surprised with my effort and that I should give Rodney my gold star, but Rodney said he didn't give me the answers, he only jogged my memory. I cut my star in half and stuck one part on him anyway.

For PE we played moon ball. It's supposed to be a cooperative game where we all have to help keep the moon (a beach ball) in space by tapping it so it bounces up. We count the taps and cooperate to make a class record.

Our record was thirty-eight hits. Ray and Vincent got thirty-four taps between them. They're bigger than the rest of us and they hog the ball. Also they don't understand the meaning of the words cooperate and tap.

The game ended when Vincent's final tap punched the ball so hard against the wall that it exploded. The ball, that is. Mrs Bright said we haven't learned anything about teamwork through the Athletics Carnival.

Thursday

Vincent is in BIG TROUBLE. Mrs Bright said he had to replace the moon ball since he wrecked ours with his irresponsible actions. So he went to the shops after school to buy a new one. But Sam says Vincent spent most of his money on bubble gum, and then he didn't have enough money for a beach ball. But he loves moon ball and really wanted to replace it. So he nicked one. He just picked one up and shoved the packet under his jumper and walked out of the shop. Then a store detective lady asked him to go back inside with her. He tried to run but she grabbed his arm and bent it back. Sam was with him but he ran off when Vincent was grabbed. He was dead scared.

This morning Vincent and his dad were in Mr Bigg's office with a policeman and Mrs Bright. We had to go to Mr Connors' room. When they came out at recess Mr Bigg and Mr Maloney looked really mad. Mrs Bright was pale and thin lipped. Vincent's face was red and splotchy and his eyes were wet. He went off with his dad and he wouldn't look at us.

The whole school is buzzing with stories. There were groups of kids in the playground, saying Vincent is going to be sent to a boys' home or be expelled.

Sam, Ray, Nigel, Rodney, Amanda and I sat and wondered what to do. And I thought how glad I was that I went straight home yesterday to do long division homework.

Friday

We tried to ring Vincent up after school but no one answered the phone. We were too scared to knock on their door because Mr Maloney can be pretty mean when he's cranky. So we tried to find a positive thought about the whole situation. We couldn't.

Then I had an idea. I said, why don't we DO something positive for Vincent. After all, he is our mate, sort of. We wrote a character reference for Vincent on my computer and ran off some copies. We took a copy to the shop manager and the store detective lady and the police station and today we gave copies to Mr Bigg and Mrs Bright. We slipped one under Vincent's front door, too, so he'd know what we'd done.

In the reference we said how Vincent used to be a bit of a thug with no social skills. But this year he had started to make friends and had been learning a lot about cooperating and being good. And if he did steal that ball it's because he was so anxious to play a cooperation game and to make up for his irresponsible action, and temptation got the better of him and he really deserves another chance, so please don't send him to jail.

The shop manager said thankyou and he would give it his consideration. The detective lady said that shop stealing is shop stealing and there is no excuse for it. Mr Bigg said our letter was all very well but Vincent stole while he was wearing his school uniform and had brought the whole school into disrepute. Mrs Bright read the reference, and turned and walked away quickly. I don't know what she thought. She didn't stop to say.

Dear Jillian,

It's a long time since I've been as proud of my students as I am of you and your friends today. Vincent is fortunate to have a group of understanding mates. I agree with you, he deserves a chance. He hasn't been expelled; his father took him home to give him thinking time.

Mrs Bright

Monday

I stayed in all weekend and hung around Mum. I looked after Paul and watched baby videos with him. I even tidied up his room. Mum said something must be wrong, and what had I broken? I told her about Vincent and everything. I don't know why I cried because it wasn't me in trouble. But she knew how I felt and gave me a hug. Even Richard listened and didn't make fun of me. When Dad came home we told him and he said that he thought Vincent would probably be let off with a stern warning if this was his first offence.

Later, when I was in bed, they both came to tuck me in and they said they were proud of me and the others, for writing the character reference.

Vincent is back at school today. He's grounded for life. If his dad is like mine, life means about a month until your constant boredness-and-idleness gets on their nerves. But that's got to be better than jail or a boys' home.

Tuesday

Yesterday after lunch Kirrily asked Mrs Bright if she could sit on the other side of the room because her mother said she wasn't to associate with criminal influences. Vincent heard and went really tense. His fists were clenched up and his teeth were grinding together. Sam and I put our hands on his arms and said to ignore her. Mrs Bright slammed her books down on her desk and said, "There are no criminal influences in this room, just children who sometimes make mistakes. We make mistakes so we can learn from them. So go back to your desk and do your work!"

I would have cheered if I dared but Mrs Bright looked like a volcano about to erupt. We all kept our heads down and looked busy. No point in tempting fate.

I wrote a note to Vincent, telling him not to let the slings and arrows of outrageous fortune get him down, but to suffer them until they go away.

He read it and scrunched it into his pocket. He didn't look at me.

Raymond isn't one to bravely suffer slings and arrows. He takes arms against seas of trouble. So when the home time bell went he put his foot out as Kirrily walked past his desk, and she tripped and bumped her nose, and it bled. When she went crying to Mrs Bright, Mrs B said it must have been an accident. Raymond is so clumsy. We didn't dare look at her. We just got out quick.

Wednesday

We're worried about Vincent. He won't play at recess and lunch and he won't talk to us. He just sits and stares at his feet. We tried giving him road kills but he said thanks and ate them, but he didn't talk. We invited him to play soccer but he said no. The others ended up going off to play, but I felt bad about leaving him. So I sat next to him and stared at my feet too. I tried to talk to him but he didn't answer. I don't know if he listened or not. I might just have been talking to myself but I kept on talking. He didn't tell me to get lost or hit me.

When the bell went and we walked up to lines Mrs Bright smiled at me.

Thursday

Another day sitting next to Vincent, yesterday. The others say I'm wasting my time because he won't answer. But I think if Vincent wanted me to go away he'd kick me. Today I read out loud while he sat and stared at his feet. It was a pretty silly book about spooks but he seemed to be listening.

After a while I stopped reading. I thought he might want to talk so I sat and looked at my feet. Every now and then he'd take a deep breath, as if he was about to speak. He never did though.

Friday

This afternoon I'm going to ask my dad to take me round to Vincent's house. I'll take him that spook story to read while he's grounded. If Mr Maloney is too cranky Dad can drive me away quickly but if he's OK I might be able to stay for a bit.

The others won't come. Nigel says he wouldn't be allowed. Sam's too scared of Vincent's dad and Ray mumbled something about having to do something else. I almost wish something would happen to stop me from having to go.

Dear Jillian,
    Well done.
    Love, Mrs Bright

Monday

Dad took me round to Vincent's. He came with me to the door and knocked. Mr Maloney answered it, and he looked a bit angry, but Dad just asked if it would be all right for me to give Vincent the book I'd promised him. Then he started chatting to Mr Maloney about football. That's the thing I really admire about Dad. He can have a conversation with anyone. Even complete strangers and scary people. They stood on the

Maloney's doorstep for ages, yakking about tries and penalties.

I went in and looked for Vincent because he didn't come out when his dad called him. Mrs Maloney was out at work at the bottle shop and Vincent's big brother was off somewhere on his motorbike. I finally found Vincent lying on their lounge staring at the ceiling.

I HAD meant to be nice to him but the sight of him lying there made me so mad. He wasn't bravely suffering the slings and arrows, and he sure wasn't fighting. My head went hot and I lost my temper. I threw the book at him and yelled that he was a great big cowardly baby, giving up and feeling sorry for himself.

He rolled over so his back was to me and covered his ears. So I yelled louder and called him a wimp. That got him going.

He turned over so quickly I thought he was going to bash me, so I backed away. But he didn't. He had tears spurting out of his eyes and his nose and he tried to say something but he couldn't because he kept breathing in huge gulps of air and hiccupping. I felt so bad for calling him names. I went over to him and patted his shoulder and said sorry. He didn't thump me so I sat down next to his feet. And waited.

A long time later, he wiped his eyes and nose on his sleeve and sat up. Then he talked. He talked for ages in little bits, in between heaving breaths. I can't write most of what he said because it was very private. He kept saying that he's always hated himself because he's stupid and rough. And this year is the first time he's ever had friends and done any schoolwork. And he was starting to feel like a normal person, and then he went and blew it and now people think he's a criminal. He said he's never cared what other people thought about him before, but he hates himself more than ever now.

I didn't know what to say. I knew how he felt because I've felt that way, too, except I do care what other people think. I sat and let him talk until he got it all out. Then I reminded him what Mrs Bright says. All people make mistakes, but the sensible ones learn from them. And, after all, Vincent still has six friends at school who know he's not a bad person.

The Maloneys are coming to our place next weekend for a barbeque. Dad and Mr Maloney have to continue their conversation about footy.

Tuesday

Now that the excitement (ha ha) of the Athletics Carnival is over, everyone is bored. There's nothing to do at playtime. Kids are starting to get annoying. The Princesses are arguing with each other. Raymond is teasing Nigel. Sam hasn't had a shower for a week. Rodney wants to play chess, but no-one will play with him because he always wins.

Mrs Bright says we're bored and idle. Mum says that too.

Last night Richard found a book of babies' names in Mum's bookshelf. Richard means "powerful ruler". So that's his excuse for pushing me around, he says. Jillian means "youthful, downy-haired one". Mum got that one right. My hair is fair and fluffy. But how could she have known it would be like that when I was born? I didn't even have hair for my first two years. Paul means "little". That's OK for now, but he's growing fast. Still, one appropriate name out of three is pretty good.

Wednesday

Mrs Bright says that bored, idle children need occupation for their minds. So she has a solution. We have to do lots of research in the school library. You'd think that would be great. But it isn't, because SHE chooses the topics. We have to find out about the three levels of government in this country and how it is run.

Amanda means "worthy of love". Nigel agrees. He wants to be her boyfriend but she said she'd beat him black and blue if he ever dares ask her.

Samuel (Sam) means "His name is God".

Sam thinks that means HIS name means God and he's getting a big head. Ray will cut him down to mortal size at playtime.

Thursday

I've decided that when I grow up I am NOT going to be a politician. Rodney wants to be one, and Nigel thinks it would be excellent to be Prime Minister and make all the rules. Rod says I should be Leader of the Opposition because I always argue. I said that's rubbish and I don't argue. Why would I want to argue? I only politely point out when people are wrong and show them their mistakes. Is that arguing?

Nigel means "dark one". Well, Nigel has reddish, mousy hair and his skin is so fair it burns and freckles on a cool day. Raymond means "mighty or wise protector". We laughed so much at that one the library teacher threw us out of the library at lunchtime. Now Nigel is cranky, because he is campaigning to be a library monitor in Year Six next year.

Friday

Detention. We had a discussion in the library about how the country should be run. Rodney and Nigel think democracy is the best way. Kirrily says we should be a proper monarchy with an Australian Queen. I said that if we had a Queen Kirrily, I'd move to Antarctica and create a republic, where I'd be president of the penguins, and probably hear more common-sense from them, too. Ray and Vincent said the army should rule because they could keep everyone under control. And a wise and mighty ruler like General Raymond could even order Princesses about.

The discussion DID get heated. Mrs Bright said we were arguing.

We have to cool off on detention.

Vincent means "conquering one". Now he's planning a military coup when he grows up.

Mrs Bright, the other teachers call you Floss. That CAN'T be your real name! I want to look up your name in the book. Will you reveal your name?

Dear Jillian

Certainly not. Teachers need some little mysteries. I won't reveal my age or phone number, either.

Another thing. You need to understand that yelling in the library does not mean discussion, no matter what you saw on Parliamentary Question Time.

Argument is using the power of words and ideas to persuade people to your way of thinking. This is something you do well when you stop taking things so personally.

Floss Bright

Monday

I'm sorry, Mrs Bright, but I can't stop taking things personally. It's the way I am. You'd take it personally too if the Princesses called you President Pest and Leader of the Argumentative Party.

Megan means "great, mighty one". It should mean "great, spiteful one". Kirrily isn't even mentioned in the name book. I'll have to give her name a meaning. Maybe "mighty irritation in the nether regions".

Mum says I'm putting myself on the level of those who give me a hard time and that's a pathetic way to behave.

Tuesday

The Princesses have declared themselves the Royal Family. They have given themselves royal titles. Of course, Kirrily is the Queen. Heir to the throne is Princess Skye. Tegan isn't talking to them because she wanted to be the main princess. They said she could be a duchess but she said that wasn't royal enough. I suggested she should declare herself Imperial Highness Tegan of Tegarnia. She told me to drop dead.

Wednesday

The Royals have invited Rodney to be their King. They made little gold crowns and they call the lunch seats their thrones. The rest of us are the peasants. They call out orders to us. The little kids bow to them and say, "Yes, your majesty."

I'm reading about the Peasants' Revolt and the English Civil War.

Thursday

I tried to tell the boys about the Peasants' Revolt and how we could overthrow the Monarchy. Raymond and Sam thought it was a great idea and said we should arm ourselves with sticks and stones and spades. But Vincent said no way is he going to do anything that could get him into trouble. One more mistake and he could get expelled.

Rodney said that in history, violence only brings bloody reprisals to the oppressed, and we need a bloodless coup. Nigel says that Rodney is a Royal Spy in the enemy camp and why doesn't he just go and sit on his Royal Throne. Sam went crazy laughing when Rodney said "bloody", because he reckons it was swearing.

I give up. I can see why the peasants never managed to overthrow their oppressors.

Friday

You can tell we're getting to the end of term. The teachers are more tired and cranky than usual and the kids are being silly, and not trying to keep their work neat. Everyone keeps talking in class and teasing other kids. The soccer games are like war zones.

I found a good name for this way of life: ANARCHY.

Jillian

Anarchy has NO rules or rulers. I am still in control of this class, tired, cranky, or not.

Mrs Bright

Monday

Last week of term, thank goodness. We're spending heaps of time doing our projects about forms of government. Not much actual work is being done, though. Some kids have managed to spend days just doing their titles.

The Royals wrote their title in a crown shape and have done a border of little crowns and sceptres and orbs round the cardboard sheet in gold and silver. Tegan is sulking because they used up her gold and silver pens and they still won't let her be a main princess. They haven't done any writing yet. Lots of little kids have brought in pictures of the Queen and Prince Charles from magazines for them to use.

Tuesday

I've got lots and lots of writing about republics but I can't think of a good way to present it. I'm supposed to be doing it now, instead of Journal. Mrs Bright says Journal isn't a priority this week. Projects are. But Journal is a good way to help you sort out your thoughts and get on task. I said so to Mrs Bright and she said I could write in my journal all lunchtime on time-out, since my thoughts need such a lot of sorting out. But she was sort of grinning when she said it. She didn't yell at me like she did at the Royals when she said that the border is the least important part of a project

Wednesday

I've wasted three sheets of cardboard. I tried drawing flags of the world's republics but that looked so boring. I traced portraits of well-known presidents but then it looked like a project about the USA so I ripped it up. Then I tried doing a big shape of the new Parliament House in Canberra until Rodney reminded me that we aren't a republic. I said "Yet."

Tegan sneered at me and I suggested to her that a Queen without a country to rule does not have a strong position to sneer from. She hit me with her sceptre. Her ruler, that is. Now she's going to be Queen of Detention. Ha, ha. It's worth the bruise.

Thursday

We had to finish our projects today. Mine looks terrible on the wall next to the Royal project. Mine is just writing. No golden borders, no glossy pictures. I told Mrs Bright that republics scorn pomp and ceremony so I avoided glittery trappings and used the plain presentation that suits the topic.

She said I am born to be a politician since I attempt to argue my way out of anything. She even grinned. The Royal Family hate me. I heard a mutter from Queen Kirrily. "Off with her head." Typical aristocracy, suppressing the free speech of the common people.

Friday

Today we're allowed to have free time all day once we finish uncompleted work and clear out our desks. Sam's still trying to do his project. Vincent's catching up on the work he missed when he was off school. Nigel and Rodney are playing computer chess because, of course, they're up-to-date with their work. Raymond's sitting trying to look innocent because he's made a pea shooter out of his biro and he's blowing spit balls at the Royals. Kirrily has one on her golden crown but she doesn't know. The Royals are decorating their books with royal symbols. Tegan has new silver and gold pens but she won't lend them to Kirrily or Skye. Only to lesser Royals like Megan and Juliet.

I think I'll help Sam with his project after I've done my long division corrections.

Term Four

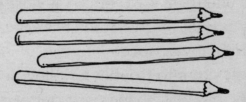

Monday

It seems as if the holidays never happened. We came back to school today and Mr Bigg made us go to Assembly. He said how we've all had a good break and have had time to rest and get the bugs out of our systems, and now we're back, we have to set our attitudes right for a long hard slog to the end of the year. We will Work until the Final Bell on the Final Day of Term and there is No Room at Flora Heights Primary School for Idlers and Slackers.

Everybody groaned.

Kirrily got into trouble for filing her finger nails. She has black nail polish on them. I said her nails look just like Sam's now and she scratched me. She's Queen of Detention today. She told Mrs Bright that I provoked her, but Mrs Bright said she saw Kirrily assault me and I had not touched her.

I asked Mrs Bright if I could go to the office to have antiseptic put on my wounds because they might turn septic, but Mrs Bright told me to not overdo the dramatics or I would end up President of the Republic of Detention.

Kirrily sent me a note saying she's going to get me if it's the last thing she ever does. I've put it in my Secrets Book. Threatening letters are a form of bullying punishable by suspension. I reminded Kirrily about that rule as I put the note in my book.

You should see the look on her face now! I love school.

Tuesday

Today I got a note from Kirrily asking me if I wanted to join the Royal Family. I could be a Duchess of the First Rank. I wrote back saying that as a republican I do not believe in outdated class systems ruled by aristocracies. I refused her offer.

Kirrily is looking anxious. She tried to smile at me at recess but her smile went wobbly. I smiled back and my smile didn't wobble. Nigel said I looked like a cat that had got the cream. Then I went to play soccer with the peasants.

School is great.

Wednesday

Last night Skye rang up and asked if I would like to go to Dance Club with her and Kirrily on Thursday afternoon. Mum was really surprised when I said no thanks. If they'd asked me in Term One, I would've thought I was in heaven. But I'm not interested in dancing now. Or in being a Princess or Royal or being popular.

Mum says I'm growing up. Richard says I might be becoming human. I told him that was more than I could say for him so he started pulling my hair. Dad sent us to our rooms and Mum said that our squabbling had changed her opinion: I haven't grown up one iota. The slings and arrows have begun to fly again.

Thursday

Tegan passed me a note this morning. It said:

Jillian James,

If a certain person gets into trouble because of a certain note there is no way you'll EVER EVER EVER be in the popular group even in High School because a certain popular group will tell everyone at High School that you're a loner loser who associates with criminals and dags and dirty boys!!!!!!!!!!!

I put the note into my Secrets Book, in an envelope labelled THREATENING LETTERS. Tegan saw me do it and smirked because her note was signed "Anonymous", so she couldn't get blamed for it. She's so stupid. Everyone knows she writes in purple biro and does little hearts instead of dots over the "i's".

Friday

The entire Royal Family is on detention today. They asked Mrs Bright if they could go into the classroom at recess to work out a dance step and she said yes. But when she went into the room to check on them, she caught them going through my desk and bag and searching through my belongings. They're in BIG trouble because some kids have lost money and stuff lately and now the Royals are under suspicion of being a gang of thieves. They're dead scared. They keep looking at me to see if I'm going to give Mrs Bright certain incriminating evidence to get them into even bigger trouble.

I'm not stupid. I had my Secrets Book with me at recess, to protect my evidence.

Mrs Bright, I do not intend to use their notes to get them into trouble unless I'm desperate. But I will keep them, because I have learned a lot about dirty tricks in politics lately and I feel more secure with a lever to use, if plots are made against me.

Vincent is stoked. He might have nicked a

beach ball once, but he's never been caught thieving in bags. He says pots shouldn't call kettles black and he's tempted to ask Mrs Bright if he can move away from criminal elements who might corrupt him. Vince is starting to like school again.

Dear Jillian,

I appreciate your feelings but do not condone your methods. Please dispose of those notes and try to get along with your classmates in a positive manner. Your mother is right. Sinking to your enemies' level when you know better is not very mature.

Mrs Bright

Monday

My classmates and I are attempting to get along in a Positive Manner. Last weekend I was invited to go to a movie with Tegan; to go for a swim in Kirrily's heated in-ground pool and to watch videos with Skye and her friends. I had a good swim at Kirrily's. Her mum is nice, but she kept asking me questions about where I live and what my dad does for a living. It was embarrassing.

I didn't go to watch videos with Skye because I knew they'd be about popstars or girls who spend their lives babysitting. But I did go to the movies with Tegan. She bought me popcorn and it was a funny movie about a kid who gets left behind at home and has a great holiday by himself. I wish that could happen to me. When the movie was over, Tegan walked home with me. She looked as if she wanted to come in but I didn't ask her. I didn't think she'd be able to cope with Paul and Richard, even though she used to belong to the ARL. She only has sisters.

When I went to bed last night I thought about the weekend. I should have felt great but I didn't. I felt sort of depressed and a bit ashamed of myself. I felt like a user. I don't think I'm politician material at all. Richard would say I'm not ruthless enough.

Tuesday

Yesterday afternoon, Mrs Bright outlined the school's plans for our torture this term. Only, they call it education. We have to participate in the School Public Speaking Competition. The grade finalists have to speak at Assembly. Then each grade winner has to represent the school at the District Interschool Public Speaking Competition Grand Final.

We had a long lesson about how to structure a speech and how to address an audience. We had to copy down notes in point form. We had to underline rules, like time limits and proper school uniform.

I got put on time-out for drawing in my book. I wasn't displaying a Positive Attitude.

Wednesday

Kirrily asked Mrs Bright what the topic for the speech would be. Mrs Bright said that since we whinge so much about being given set topics for research, we would be happy to know that there was no set topic for the Public Speaking.

We have to give a speech about something of personal significance to the speaker.

I can't decide if that's good or terrible. We thought it was a pain getting set topics for research last term but I did learn a lot about government which I would never have bothered to learn about otherwise. And I don't want to speak about something personally significant to me. It would be like cutting your head open to let someone see how your brain works. Or standing naked in front of everyone.

Thursday

The Princesses are sooooo excited about the Public Speaking Competition. They've got sooooo many topics, they can't decide what to talk about. Raymond absolutely refuses to write a speech about himself. He says his private life is his and no-one else's.

Nigel has decided to speak about the uses

and abuses of libraries, and Rodney is trying to find a way to make his excitement about Information Technology equally exciting for listeners.

My feelings are like Raymond's. I don't want to hold my secret hopes and dreams up to public ridicule. I'd rather do a speech about What I Did In My Holidays or What I Want To Do When I Grow Up.

Poor Sam. He reckons he's got nothing significant in his life worth speaking about. Vincent can only think about his shameful past. He wants to thump whoever thought of making Public Speaking compulsory.

Friday

I never thought I would EVER copy an idea of the Princesses. But today I did. They were sitting on their thrones at recess and they had a big sheet of paper. They were brainstorming. They didn't KNOW that's what they were doing, but it was. They kept thinking and calling out ideas that were personally significant to their group and Skye wrote them down in orange pen on the sheet. Then they worked out which girl should write about which topic.

Tegan told me to stop spying on them and to go and play boy games with my dirty friends. Kirrily said I could sit with their group if I wanted to and she tried to smile at me but her eyes weren't smiling. She looked so uncomfortable that I started to feel a little sorry for her and I almost told her not to worry about the notes. But then I decided that Kirrily trying to be nice is a lot easier to live with than Kirrily being normal, so I didn't put her out of her misery after all. I just said no thanks, I was just off to join my FRIENDS.

As I walked away I heard Kirrily blowing Tegan up for being mean to me. I went to Mrs Bright to ask if I could get a sheet of paper, and all the Princesses watched me talking to her. They looked scared.

I could become accustomed to having power over others.

Jillian,

Do you seriously call this behaviour POSITIVE?

Mrs Bright

Monday

We all met in the tree house on Saturday to brainstorm ideas for our speeches. In the end we had:

Rodney: *Computers, Information Technology and Me.*

Sam: *Soccer for Fun and Friendship.*

Raymond: *Martial Arts for Fitness and Self-Defence.*

Amanda: *Girls, the Greatest Sportsmen?*

Nigel: *Libraries, Their Uses and Abuses.*

Jillian: *Slings And Arrows Of Outrageous Fortune, To Fight or to Suffer?*

We spent all Sunday morning brainstorming ideas to put into our speeches. Amanda reckons she'll be OK because she knows her subject. She lives it.

I helped Sam. We looked up a book of Richard's, called *Soccer for Beginners*, so he could get clear about rules.

Nigel and Rodney both had a similar problem: that was, how to cut all their ideas down to the allowable length. Raymond might need help because all his ideas seem to be violent.

Poor old Vincent hasn't got ANY ideas. None of our suggestions appealed to him. He almost thumped Nigel when he suggested "Honesty Is The Best Policy". Nigel can be very tactless. I suppose that's because no-one is tactful to him, when they tell him to drop dead.

I'm going to start on my speech tonight after tea and my bath, and after I read Paul the story I promised him.

Tuesday

Today I'm really tired. I stayed up half the night trying to think of a speech. I couldn't find a way to structure it. In the end I made a list of every sling and arrow that has been cast at me since Year Three. The list was about a hundred pages long but I still didn't have an idea of how to get the speech going.

Then Mum made me go to bed because it was a school night. I dreamed all night about being trapped in a school full of Kirrilys and Skyes, and everywhere I turned they hissed that I was unpopular and ugly and clumsy and Nigellated.

When I woke up this morning I was tired and sad, like I used to be when I was a loner. I think my dream was still inside me.

Wednesday

Today at recess and lunch I sat with Vincent and Sam and discussed speeches. Nigel, Rodney and Amanda went off somewhere to publish theirs. We timed Sam's speech and it only went for one minute and six seconds. So we thought of more things, like how soccer is fun and teamwork builds friendships.

While he was rewriting, I told Vincent about my dream. He didn't know me when I was a loner; he never noticed I existed, that is. So I told him what it used to be like for me. He got really mad and looked as if he was going to thump the Princesses, but I told him not to because he'd end up in trouble and they can't hurt me anymore.

He asked me why and I told him half the truth. I didn't tell him about the incriminating letters because I've decided not to use them (ninety-five percent decided, anyway); I told Vincent how they used to get at me because I didn't have friends, and that made me vulnerable, but they can't hurt me now since I do have friends and now I feel confident and good about myself. I think he understood what I was saying. He didn't say much. He just hummed and stared at his feet. I think he was thinking.

Thursday

Sam's speech is almost three minutes long now. Only sixty seconds more to make up. He's so happy. He's never done a speech before. He's never been able to think of ideas or write things down. He doesn't expect to win, because Rodney probably will, but he feels good and Mrs Bright will be pleased that he's made the effort.

I'll try to get my speech done tonight. Probably.

Friday

When Mum came in to turn my light out last night, she saw all the bits of torn and crumpled paper on the floor and she could see I'd been crying. She sat on the bed and asked how she could help. I told her about the Public Speaking Competition and how everybody else except Vincent and I have ideas and speeches already, and I couldn't make my only idea work.

She listened to what I did have written down. Then she sat looking at her fingernails and twisting her ring around her finger. So I knew she didn't like it either. I asked her what was wrong and how could I fix it. She took a deep breath as if she was trying to find courage then burst out that she didn't like what I had written because it sounded petty and vindictive and that's not my true self.

I ripped it up and cried myself to sleep.

I don't think I'll do a speech. I don't have an interesting life and there's nothing worth writing about.

Dear Jillian,

You WILL write a speech! Just stop procrastinating and write about something you know.

Mrs Bright

Monday

This is spooky. Mum asked me on Friday and again on Saturday how my speech was progressing. I kept saying I'd get around to it as soon as I got an idea. When she asked me again on Saturday afternoon and I said I'd start it after dinner she yelled at me. She said, "Stop worrying about big ideas! You're procrastinating! Write about something simple. Something you know!"

Anybody would think she'd been talking to Mrs Bright.

I got sent to my bedroom and told I couldn't come out until I could show significant progress.

While I was lying on the bed trying to

balance my pencil by its point on my fingertip, I heard Dad ask Richard when he was going to mow the lawn like he'd promised, two weeks ago. Richard yelled out "I'm going to, Dad! But I have to do this homework now. I'll do it later, OK?"

And that's when inspiration hit me.

I spent all day Sunday writing. I only had fourteen snack and toilet breaks, and Paul only got three stories before Mum chased me back to work.

Vincent has an idea for his speech as well, but he's keeping his topic secret, like me. He said not to worry, there's nothing violent or nasty or criminal in it. That made Raymond sit up and listen. He's asked us to help him get the inappropriate bits out of his draft at lunchtime. Raymond actually wants a good report this term. If I hadn't thought of my topic on Saturday I could write about Small Miracles.

Tuesday

Now everyone is keeping their speeches secret and trying to spy on everyone else to find out what theirs is about.

Kirrily acted friendly and asked me what my speech is about and I told her it's called "How To Win Friends And Influence People." Tegan said it must be a really short speech then, if it contained all I knew about the subject. So I said no, I'd learned a lot from her and her friends over the years.

There must have been something in my tone of voice, or the incriminating letters haven't been forgotten, because Kirrily's looking dead scared again. Talk about a guilty conscience!

I asked Kirrily what her speech is about and she said it's about her hobbies. Then she said, "You know—singing and dancing, I mean. Not anything else! I . . . um . . . I want to be an entertainer . . . you know. . ." and she walked off quickly.

I wonder what she imagines I was thinking

her hobbies might be. Letter writing, maybe? Or character assassination?

Wednesday

Last night I practised my speech for Mum and Dad. They LIKE it. Mum said I'd finally found a topic I could talk about authoritatively. Dad said it was a masterpiece of understatement. Even Richard listened and made a few suggestions. Helpful ones, I mean. He must have liked the speech too, because he said it was worthy of him. He's sooo modest.

I can't wait until next Monday when we do our speeches in class.

The rumours going round are getting wilder. Rodney and Nigel and I started most of them but some appeared from nowhere. Rumour says that Skye is giving a speech on the "Philosophy of Barbie Dolls and How to Achieve Barbiehood." Vincent is supposed to be speaking on the topic "Fifty ways to Flatten A Princess." Nigel is supposed to be speaking on

"The Joys Of Nigellation" and Raymond will tell us what he would do if he ran the world, in "A Lesson On Anarchy".

Thursday

Mr Bigg reminded us about being well groomed and well presented for our speeches, so we've been brushing our teeth and combing our hair. Our fingernails have been trimmed. I asked Rodney how they would see our nails if we're up on stage and he said judges have eagle eyes. Sam is showering every night and his skin gets paler each time. His hair is actually blondish. We've just discovered that. And the potatoes in his ears have been dug out.

Mum even found my proper school shoes and Dad polished them. They're a bit tight but they'll have to do. And Mum finally gave in and sewed up my tunic hem. I never did get round to it.

I'm doing another practice tonight. After the vet show on TV.

Friday

When Mum dragged me out of bed this morning she said I'd better not practise my speech again before our class performance. She reckons I can say it well enough now and practising is making me nervous. I was dreaming all night about not being able to get to school on Public Speaking day. In my dream I kept losing my speech, then my clothes, then I was walking in the wrong direction. And all the time Richard's voice kept saying, 'You're doing this deliberately! You don't WANT to do a speech, do you?'

I'm tired. I don't want to do my maths. Or spelling. I just want to sleep a long dreamless sleep.

Dear Jillian,
    I know that if you've had a good, restful weekend, you'll be just fine.
    Mrs Bright

Monday

The BIG DAY.

   I'm shaking all over. Hope I'm on first. Get it over with.

Tuesday

The BIG DAY has come and gone. We did our speeches in the assembly hall, with just our class. Kirrily talked about singing and dancing and the thrill it gives her. The Princesses LOVED it. Actually they ALL did speeches about their hobbies, which are mainly singing and dancing. After the fifth speech where we had to look at a large photo or a video of the speaker in a concert, it became boring. But that was OK because it made everyone else's sound interesting.

   The whole class stood up and clapped when Sam did his speech. Mrs Bright couldn't make her throat work and her eyes were wet. She went to Sam and hugged him. He yelled

"Yuk!" and wriggled away. But he had a grin right across his face when he sat down.

After recess, Nigel and then Rodney had their turns. Naturally they were brilliant. Well prepared and well presented. And Amanda was really confident and interesting. Kid after kid got up to speak. Every time Mrs Bright called out a name my heart jumped. Then the lunch bell rang. There were only two more speeches to be given. Vincent's and mine.

I couldn't eat my lunch. I felt sick.

When we came back in, I asked Mrs Bright if I could go home. She laughed and said, "No way!" Vincent had to go first. His mysterious speech turned out to be all about Friendship. He got up and spoke about this year and how he was an angry kid. Then he made friends with Sam, Raymond, Nigel and Rodney and me. He said how we had helped him through schoolwork and the Athletics Carnival, and how he'd started to enjoy learning things. Then he said he had really learned about the value of friendship when he made a big mistake and shoplifted because he wanted to be part of the group. He said the best friend a kid could ever have supported him and helped him face the world again when he just wanted to curl up and die. That friend was Jillian and thanks, JJ.

Then he sat down and stared at his feet.

There was total silence in the room. I felt as if everyone was staring at me. I don't know if they were, because my face was hidden in my arms on the back of the chair in front of me. It wasn't because I'm ashamed of crying. I was nervous about my speech.

Then Raymond yelled "Good onya Vince!" and everyone clapped and cheered. Mrs Bright had to blow her nose and clear her throat a few times. Then it was my turn. I wanted to die.

But I didn't. I walked to the stage and started. I croaked. I tried again and this time I gulped. I almost asked Mrs Bright if I could do it another day, but as I looked to her I caught Vincent's eye. His eye seemed to be saying, "Don't you dare, Jillian James."

So I did my speech.

We find out the finalists on Friday.

Wednesday

The other night Mum and Dad asked me how the Public Speaking went and I said it was all right. I told them how good Rodney and Nigel were and how everyone cheered for Sam. They all laughed, even Richard, when I described the five identical Princess speeches. Then Richard did a Princess speech that had us rolling on the floor.

But I didn't tell them about Vincent's speech. Some things are too personal to talk about.

Thursday

Yesterday we were all trying to guess who the Year Five finalists will be. Everyone reckons Rodney is sure to be one. Some say Nigel will, too, because his speech was really good. But other kids say that Nigel doesn't grab an audience's attention. We'd like Sam to get a chance but he doesn't want it. Vincent threatens to thump anyone who even mentions his speech, so we don't think Mrs Bright will dare choose him. I hope she doesn't choose him. His speech was great, but it shouldn't be repeated.

The Princesses say Kirrily is Absolutely SURE to be a finalist because she had videos and photos and was soooo good. Kirrily and Tegan said I don't have a snowball's chance in hell of being chosen. I pick peculiar subjects and the speech was supposed to be about something of personal significance! Raymond tripped Kirrily up when she was walking away and he said, "Oh, dear! How clumsy of me! I DO apologize, Kirrily. My feet are SOOO big." So she couldn't run crying to Mrs Bright.

Friday

I got seven out of ten for long divisions today. I got twenty out of twenty for my spelling. Mrs Bright has made us wait all day for the big announcement. She keeps smirking. I used to like it when a teacher smiled but not today. Kirrily has smirked all morning, as well.

Most of us just got on with our work because we knew we didn't stand a chance of being selected. Raymond reckons only teachers' pets get chosen.

2.30 pm NEWS FLASH! Raymond is wrong. The Year 5 Finalists are:

Rodney

Nigel

Jillian

I think I'm going to be sick. I think Kirrily is too. She's gone green.

Dear Jillian,

Congratulations! Your speech will entertain the Assembly next Tuesday. Relax. Enjoy the experience.

Mrs Bright

Monday

We went to a restaurant last Friday night to celebrate. My parents were ecstatic about me being a finalist. Richard was actually nice to me. We had Italian food and bought fancy ice-creams on the way home.

It was the best weekend. The boys all came round and we played soccer and things to keep Rodney's and Nigel's and my minds off speeches. None of us really minds which of us becomes Year Five champion because we're friends. Besides, Rodney had a great topic and spoke the best, so we know who'll win.

Tuesday

Speeches will be held all day today. Every grade has three speakers and we need to keep taking breaks to quieten the little kids down. My stomach is churning and my heart is thumping. I wish I could do my speech tomorrow. Or next year.

Year Five's turn next. Nigel, then Rodney. Then me.

JILLIAN JAMES, 5B
MY SPEECH

I lay on my bed, thinking. I had almost got the point of my pencil to balance on my fingertip when Mum bashed on the door and yelled, "Jillian! How's that speech going?"

When my heart returned to its normal position, from my throat, where it had leapt in fright, I yelled back, "Fine, Mum! Er . . . I'm just thinking about it! I think I've got an idea coming!"

I jumped up and sat at my desk and surveyed my list of ideas. A blank page.

Next night I sat at my desk again staring at the blank sheet. My seven pencils lay, freshly sharpened. At both ends. They were all now 10 cm long and lay silently begging to be the one to be picked up and made use of.

Mum burst in. "Now, then. How's that speech going?"

Confession time. It couldn't be avoided.

"Mum, I just can't come to grips with it. I can't even think of a topic. Maybe after I have a shower. . . "

"Oh, no, you don't! Stop that procrastinating! Sit down and WRITE! Forget about fancy topics. Write about something you know well!"

And that, boys and girls, is the reason I am here today, to tell you about the Subtle Art Of Procrastination.

The dictionary will inform you that procrastination is the act of putting off the things you must do until later. Poets through the ages have whined that procrastination is the thief of time. Parents and teachers constantly cry "procrastination" in accusing voices when you haven't done what THEY decided you should do.

I beg to differ. From my personal experience over 11 years of sustained observation and practice, I can assure you that procrastination is actually a fiendishly effective method of GAINING time for doing the things you

REALLY want to do. In fact, procrastination is really another word for prioritisation, a trait highly rated by time and motion experts.

Let me illustrate my point.

I come from a long line of procrastinators. My parents waited until they were quite elderly—thirty—before they started a family. They were waiting for the right time. Then my brother wasn't born until he was three weeks overdue—and the doctor forced him out. He was waiting for the right time.

At my house, procrastination is an art form. A family tradition. A way of life.

We call my big brother Gonna. He is in a constant state of gonna start things. He's in Year Nine now. He's gonna start working seriously at school this year. When Mum asks how he expects to get a good report he says "Oh, Mum, have faith in me. I'm gonna study hard at exam time. I'll be right." His job is to put out the garbage. Every time, Mum has to tell him to do it and every time his answer is, "Oh, yeah, I'm gonna do it after dinner, Mum! Give me a break!"

We call our little brother Wendy. A bit rude to name a little boy that, but it suits him. He's pretty useless and gets in the way when we have to clean up. Mum and Dad say, "Never mind, when he gets older he'll be able to help, too. Just now he's too little."

And me? Am I a Gonna or a Wendy? No. They call me Justa. I am the one who has refined procrastination—I mean prioritisation—to the art form it is at our house. I have hobbies and interests, needs and wants, which rarely match the demands adults impose on me, like mealtimes, bath, homework, bedtime. I'm always searching for time for the things I need. Like reading, playing, thinking.

Mum has a spooky knack of calling me to dinner when I'm in the middle of a chapter. "Jillian! Dinner!"

'OK!' I yell back. And keep reading.

Five minutes later, "Jillian! Your dinner's getting cold!"

"Justa minute! I'm coming!" I reply. I can do it without losing my place.

Five minutes later she'll barge in and say

"Didn't you hear me? Dinner's ready!" and I'll get up, saying, "I was just coming, Mum."

You see? Ten valuable minutes gained and you have the chapter finished instead of choking over broccoli.

It's a very useful technique for seeing the TV shows you like, too. Parents always seem to remember homework just as the show you've been waiting for is starting.

"Oh, Jillian! Have you got homework?" Obviously Dad suspects I do, because Mrs Bright is a homework fanatic.

"Um, no. I don't think so, Dad." Eyes glued to the screen to show him there's something IMPORTANT on. Five minutes gained. Now you know if it's a repeat or not, so you can calculate how much effort needs to be put in here.

Then he remembers. "Well, how can you be sure you don't?"

"Um, well, I'll check. Just a minute. I'll look during the ads."

Another five minutes gained.

"JILLIAN! Do you have homework or not?"

"Oh, Dad, just a bit. Just a minute. I can do it straight after this show finishes."

If you put your mind to it, you can gain a whole evening's viewing and reading pleasure without wasting any more time than is absolutely necessary on dinner and homework. Then they'll say, "It's late! Go to bed!" and you can reply "But I have to do my maths!" and sure as eggs they'll put their parental foot down and say, "No time for that! You should have thought of that before, so you must face the consequences! Shower and bed!"

A very quick shower and into bed for thinking time. Of course, they assume you're sleeping.

Just imagine how the world could be, if people used this technique wisely. What if the man who was ordered to drop the bomb over Hiroshima said, "Justa minute. I'll do it after my coffee break." The bomb would have dropped into the sea and killed a few fish, perhaps. But there would have been 200 000 grateful—and alive—people.

And what if Henry VIII had said, "Anne, I'm gonna have your head chopped off tomorrow. I'm too busy today." He might have forgotten his murderous intentions and ended up with only two wives. At least five grateful women there!

So next time your teachers or parents accuse you of wasting time, remember: to procrastinate is NOT to delay, tarry, loiter, kill time or dilly-dally. Oh, no. It is to make time, save time, prioritise, keep your shirt on, see which way the cat jumps, which way the wind blows, and, in the end, save unnecessary labour in the pursuit of the finest things in life.

And now, I must get round to writing that speech I'm meant to do. You know, the one about something of personal significance to me. I AM gonna write one, you know. Just as soon as I get home. And have a snack. And change. And read. Really. I'll get on to it tonight. If I get a good idea. Maybe.

Wednesday

When I got home yesterday Mum wanted to know how my Public Speaking went. I told her that I don't really know. The teachers all seemed to have coughing fits while I was talking and the kids didn't clap politely like they did for Nigel and Rodney and the Year Six kids. They sort of cheered, but that might have been set off by Ray and Sam and Vince. Or more likely, because mine was the last speech before Year Six, who are always good. We won't know until Friday who the grade winners are.

Richard said the humour in my speech was probably too subtle for them but Dad said it had the subtlety of a sledgehammer. Anyway, it's over with and I got a merit card for being a grade finalist.

I slept like a log last night.

Thursday

I must be growing up. Now I can understand why my mum and my teacher say, "OK, joke's over. Give it a rest!" Teachers keep coming up to me in the playground and making comments like, "Oh, Jillian, there's a paper on the ground. Will you pick it up—in justa minute?"

Or, "Jillian, wen de bell goes, would you take this message round? Ha, ha!" Mrs Bright even said she's gonna give us extra homework—when she gets around to organizing it.

I'm starting to wish I'd never written that speech. Three words I never intend to use again are gonna, justa and wendy.

Friday

Mr Bigg called assembly this morning.

The good part was, we missed our spelling and maths tests.

The bad part was—well, a mixed blessing.

He wanted to announce the grade winners who get to present their speeches at the District Interschool Public Speaking Competition.

Mr Bigg started with Year Three. Then Year Four. When he got to announcing the Year Five winner I had already leant across Sam and Nigel so I could be the first to congratulate Rodney. So when Mr Bigg said "Jillian James" I fell into their laps and rolled on to the floor.

Mr Bigg said, "Jillian is gonna come up onto the stage with the other winners. Wen de other children help her up off the floor where she is resting. Justa minute while she recovers from her shock."

I think I want to die.

Dear Jillian,
Hold off dying until after the competition! Congratulations.
Mrs Bright

Monday

The weekend was good. Another trip to a restaurant, and everyone proud of me—even Richard, who says I should do more good things because the parents forget to nag at him, and take us out to dinner.

Mum didn't make me clean up my room and Dad said I could use his computer printer any time.

But I didn't use it much. I still feel sick.

Tuesday

I don't think I can go through with this competition thing. Nigel won't talk to me. He really thought he had it won. He told Amanda who told Raymond who told Sam who told me that I won by sucking up to teachers.

Yeah, right, Nigel—as if I could beat you at YOUR game. But I won't say that to him. It's weird. In Term One I'd have done anything to make Nigel go away. But now I'd rather have

220

my friends than lose them by winning a stupid speech competition.

Even though Mum and Mrs Bright are pleased with me.

Wednesday

I was expecting Rodney to hate me too, but he said I deserved to win. We talked about it and agreed that his speech was better constructed and more intelligent, and his speaking was clearer than mine.

So I asked why did I win, then, and not him?

He says I've got something he hasn't got. But he didn't know how to put it into words.

Thursday

Kirrily and Company have asked Nigel to join their new club. It's called the Anti-JJ Club. They asked him in front of me. I couldn't be bothered feeling upset. I don't care if they are anti Jillian James. That's something I'm used to. But I will feel sad if Nigel joins them. Even if he hates me, he doesn't deserve them.

Friday

They've asked Rodney, too. He laughed and said they had to be joking. He said he is my greatest admirer. Sam and Vincent and Raymond agreed with him and Ray said that Princesses should be locked up in high towers with no doors. We all played soccer at lunch.

After lunch Nigel came over and said that he had decided he didn't want to be part of Kirrily's fan club and could he please be my friend again. I said he always had been my friend, ever since Term One, though he nearly blew it over a stupid speech.

But I still feel sick and I wish Rodney had whatever it is that he says I've got and he doesn't. I'd rather have a settled stomach.

Dear Jillian,

Butterflies in your tummy are the effect of adrenalin. Look that up in your dictionary. Adrenalin will help you. And while you're at it, the word Rodney needs is charisma. Look that one up too.

Love, Mrs B

Monday

Adrenalin: hormone secreted by adrenal glands, affecting circulation and muscular action; causing excitement and stimulation.

Richard says adrenalin is important for survival because it speeds up your reflexes when you're in danger. So? Does this mean I can run away quickly if I fall up the steps to the stage? Or will it make me talk faster so I get the speech over in half the time?

The Competition is on Thursday. All the grade finalists are allowed to come to the town hall to support their representatives.

Nigel and Rodney are going to be my cheer squad. But if Nigel whistles, I'll never talk to him again. Mum won't give me a headache tablet for my stomach. She says it won't cure adrenalin. The only cure for that is to put my mind to doing a good job on the day.

Tuesday

Charisma: divinely conferred power or talent; capacity to inspire followers with devotion and enthusiasm.

ME? With divine power? You've got to be kidding, Mrs Bright! Richard and the boys fell about laughing when we looked that word up. Richard said the only divine power I've got is to get uglier each year.

But I do agree with him; I can't have charisma. If I had charisma I'd have been a Princess since Year Three. And I would never have made friends with Sam and Nigel and Raymond and Rodney and Vincent and Amanda.

I don't need charisma. I have friends.

And I still feel sick. I have adrenalin overdose.

Wednesday

The Big Day is tomorrow. Mum is washing and ironing my tunic today, so I'm wearing my sports tracksuit. Mrs Bright actually said that's excusable!!!

Raymond gave me a bag of Siamese twins to keep me going. Vincent lent me his lucky penknife to "slash the opposition". I'm positive he doesn't mean it literally. Almost. Kirrily and Skye are making sure I notice them NOT noticing me as they walk past, arm in arm.

I'm too pumped up with adrenalin to care.

Friday

Mr Bigg called Assembly today. My ears are still ringing and burning and my shoulders are still sore, from the cheering and embarrassment and back-slapping when he announced to the school who won the Year Five Division of the Interschool Public Speaking Competition. EVERYONE cheered, even Kirrily and Company. This makes up for everything. Friendship pins, Princesses, war cries, nasty notes and teachers' moods just don't seem like slings and arrows any more. Not even my high-jump record.

I don't feel sick any more either. Just very relieved and very, very tired. I'm going to sleep all weekend.

Dear Jillian,
     I KNEW you'd do it! Well done!
     Love, Mrs Bright

Monday

The term has nearly ended and nobody noticed it happening. Mrs Bright said we've been caught napping. So this week we're frantically doing last-minute assessment tasks and doing practice for Presentation Day.

The teachers are stressed. The kids are on holidays in their heads already.

Tuesday

Today's tests:
* Maths mentals
* Maths problems
* Spelling (one hundred words)
* Reading aloud

Other Activities:
* Singing, while sitting
* Singing, while standing up

Wednesday

Tests:
* Reading comprehension
* Punctuation and grammar
* Government

Other Activities:

- ★ Detention for yawning loudly during tests
- ★ Ordeal by voices:
  practising the words sitting
  practising the words standing
  doing it all again; in tune, and in
  UNISON this time!
- ★ Mr Bigg yelling at Year Six kids for getting too big for their boots.

Thursday

Tests:

- ★ Language and Vocabulary
- ★ Written Expression
- ★ Science and Technology

Other Activities:

- ★ A complete run-through of Presentation Day Program from go to whoa, without the announcements of prize winners, but with the inclusion of several talks about behaviour.

Friday

We are all sitting at our desks, working quietly on pain of death.

Mrs Bright gave us a heap of worksheets with Christmas puzzles on them. We have to do the puzzles and colour in the pictures. If we have a problem with that we have to go through our books and complete any unfinished work from the year. Just as long as we don't bother Mrs Bright. She's sitting at her desk, concentrating madly on her assessment records.

Personally I don't think she cares very much what we do. She just wants to get our reports done to give to Mr Bigg. He has to read them and sign them all, and he wants to do it over the weekend. We get them next week. After Presentation Day is over.

Kirrily and the Princesses are passing notes to each other. Raymond and Vincent are playing Battleships on the back of their Santa sheets. Rodney and Nigel have finished their worksheets and are playing chess with a miniature magnetic set. Rodney's got three wins and Nigel has two so far. Sam's reading a book. Mrs Bright saw but she pretended she didn't. She looked away, smiling. I'm writing this. I'll miss my journal next year.

Dear Jillian,
 There's no reason to miss your journal after this year is over. A journal-writing habit can be lifelong and very rewarding. If you were an adult I'd consider showing you my diary! But you might be shocked to see how much my thoughts are like yours.
 G Bright

Monday

G Bright? Come ON, Mrs B! Are you a Gabrielle? A Gretchen? A Gail? Or are you Georgette? Gilda? Gloria? I searched the baby name book this weekend to guess your name.

Is it Gertrude (Spear maiden)? Or Galadriel (Queen of the elves)? Or Galiana (Supreme one)?

My bet is Galiana because the meaning suits you.

A certain person who shall not be named here reckons Gladys (lame) might be more suitable. Perhaps they're right. Remember the Marbles Incident. Or, maybe, Geraldine (mighty with a spear)—if you think back to the Rulers Ban.

After lunch we're having ANOTHER practice, mainly because we don't know the words to the songs yet.

Tuesday

We have spent this morning cleaning out the dead bits of paper, green sandwiches, half-sucked lollies and broken rulers from our desks and all the class bookshelves and cupboards.

Our bags are stuffed with the year's art,

our projects and craft, and anything Mrs Bright threw out and we nicked back out of the bin. I scored some perfectly good paper, which is only mouse-eaten on one corner. We aren't allowed to take our books home until Friday.

Tomorrow is Presentation Day. And REPORTS!

Thursday is Class Party Day. We're having pizza, delivered. Then we're having cans of fizzy drink, and watermelon and ice blocks. We all had to bring in five dollars, but our mums are happy to pay up because they don't have to make party food.

Friday is clean-up day. Most kids "forget" to come that day. Mum always makes me come. You always know who's planning not to come on the last day. They're the ones who sneak their books into their bags on Thursday afternoon.

Thursday

This is my last entry in this journal. The parents were so pleased with my report last night they said they'd let me stay home on Friday, since it's the last day.

I have improved in Effort AND Achievement in all my subjects. Even maths! Which means Mrs Bright really deserves to be a Galiana. Or even a Gloria (glorious). Because I really, truly, have tried to conquer maths this year. And she's helped me.

Yesterday was a day full of surprises. And I thought that nothing would surprise me after the year I've had.

FIRST SURPRISE

We all managed to stand up straight and still and remembered ALL the words and tunes. Now I know what the expression "visibly relieved" means. Mr Bigg was.

SECOND SURPRISE

Rodney won the Maths and Science Outstanding Achievement prizes for Year Five. (Well, that's no surprise, except for Nigel who's always won them in the past.)

Amanda won Senior Girls' Sportsperson. (No surprises there.)

Sam got Most Improved Student! We all cheered and cheered. Mrs Bright told Vincent and Raymond that they were close to winning that one. They were stoked. They've never been close to a school prize in their lives. Sam looks like he's had Christmas already. Goodonya, Supreme One!

I won the trophy for the Interschool Public Speaking Competition Overall Champion, so I was Christmassy, too.

Then they called out the winner of the Outstanding English in Year Five prize.

Jillian James.

I was amazed. I was speechless.

Then came the second biggest surprise of the day.

THIRD SURPRISE

They announced the Senior Citizenship Trophy winner. That's even bigger than Sports prizes.

Jillian James.

I was so stunned that I still don't know how I got from my seat to the stage. I only woke up when I fell up the steps. But noone laughed. They cheered me. And the loudest cheer was from Vincent.

When I went back to my seat I saw my parents in the audience. Mum was blubbering into her hanky. Dad seemed to be busy polishing his glasses with his hanky. But I saw him sniff.

And the BIGGEST surprise?

FOURTH, BIGGEST and LAST SURPRISE of the day, the term, the year. . .

Well, actually that was at home time when the reports were handed out. Mrs Bright handed out Christmas cards to us. In my card she wished me all the best in the future. And she signed the card with her full name.

GILLIAN Bright!!!

See you next year, Mrs Bright. And thanks for this year.